W9-AQL-112

MOUSTAPHA'S ECLIPSE

Winner

of the

Drue Heinz Literature Prize

1988

MOUSTAPHA'S ECLIPSE

Reginald McKnight

UNIVERSITY OF PITTSBURGH PRESS

Published by the University of Pittsburgh Press, Pittsburgh, Pa. 15260

Feffer and Simons, Inc., London
Manufactured in the United States of America

Library of Congress Cataloging-in-Publication Data

McKnight, Reginald, 1955-
Moustapha's eclipse / Reginald McKnight.
p. cm.
Contents: Mali is very dangerous—First I look at the purse—Peaches—Who big Bob?—Uncle Moustapha's eclipse—Gettin to be like the studs—The voice—The honey boys—How I met Idi at the Bassi Dakaru Restaurant—Rebirth.
ISBN 0-8229-3589-9
I. Title.
PS3563.C3833M6 1988
813′.54—dc19

88-6408
CIP

"First I Look at the Purse" originally appeared in *Players*, "Mali Is Very Dangerous" is reprinted from *The Massachusetts Review*, © 1986, the Massachusetts Review, Inc., and "Uncle Moustapha's Eclipse" first appeared in *Prairie Schooner*.

—to Big Daddy

Contents

MOUSTAPHA'S ECLIPSE

Mali Is Very Dangerous

IN my first few days in Senegal I quickly learned to fend off illness, culture shock and flies, but I had no prophylactic against M.D.—Moustapha Diole, a very gentle but underhanded soul who peddled to tourists on N'Gor Beach. I met M.D. on my second day in the country near N'Gor Village, a labyrinthine stone crab surrounded by hotels, bush, and endless cobalt blue water. On that day he stripped me of one hundred dollars in less than ten minutes for some very chintzy-looking "authentic African art." Fortunately for me, one hundred dollars was all the cash I carried that day.

There I was, a twenty-six-year-old graduate anthropologist, relatively well read in the folklore, history, art, and contemporary literature of West Africa. I had been given a very handsome chunk of research money by a reputable, if not redoubtable, East Coast university in order to study African market systems. In less than thirty-six hours in-country, I found myself bamboozled by a snaggletoothed, illiterate old man into buying trinkets a kleptomaniac would scorn. It wasn't my squandering the money that disturbed me so much as it was M.D.'s deftness at convincing me that junk was jewelry, trash was treasure, up was down. A lesson in smart shopping I won't soon forget.

I ran into M.D. again one night several weeks later on N'Gor Beach while strolling, repeating French phrases to myself. I suppose, because M.D. had had such tremendous luck with me at our first meeting, he seemed expressly happy to see me. "Ahhh, here comes the original mark," he must have been thinking. He took my hand, shook it like we were old school chums, and without letting go, told me in his most eloquent Franco-American pidgin he wanted to introduce me to his wife and kids. I figured his intent was to let his family meet, up close, the sap who had tripled his monthly income in seconds flat. His wife was very sick, he told me, but he wanted me to meet her just the same. He led me down the beach, clutching my hand as if I were his steady.

What's funny about Islamic countries like Senegal is that you rarely see men holding women's hands. You see men hold men's hands, and women hold women's hands. It's an oddly pleasant custom, man and man, woman and woman, strolling hand in hand—not that I personally cared for the custom though. The best I could muster was an aesthetic, and distant, appreciation.

M.D. tried pulling me toward his place as if I'd heartily agreed to come along. I told him I was busy, that I had a lot of research to attend to, that I was tired, wanted to turn in early. He grinned, pretending not to understand. Then he told me he wanted me to meet a "young girl" before going to his home in N'Gor. I felt myself put up a little less resistance, but resisted nevertheless. I simply wasn't interested in meeting his young girl, his old wife, or anybody else. I told him so. He gave me this long, hurt-looking face with sad-dog eyes. "You are my friend?" he asked. "Yes," I said. "The best friend I ever had."

"Please, my friend, come. Come see my wife. She very sick."

A dozen snappy comebacks occurred to me, but I couldn't bring myself to say anything nasty. "Please come with me," he said. And I relented, thinking, I need an enemy out here like I need a sand sandwich. So, I let M.D. lead me by the hand to a bar at the Diarama Hotel. Once there he introduced me to the young girl, his sister, he told me. He then, very casually, asked me whether I wanted her. I guess any normal man would have. Tall, big butt, mahogany eyes and skin, rice-white teeth, breasts Solomon couldn't describe. A killer dame. I wasn't the least bit interested. At the time, I was trying to remain faithful to my girlfriend Lillian, which ended up, ten months later, like waiting for an order of fish and chips at a Taco Bell.

I wasn't interested in M.D.'s "sister," but I was certainly intrigued. Maybe mystified would be a better word, for it seemed to me that M.D. was offering me the whore for nothing. Now, Senegalese whores go for a lot less than they do in the States. Two, three bucks a round when I was in Senegal. I kept asking M.D. how much this one would cost and he kept saying, "You are my friend. You are my friend." I wasn't sure whether he was talking discount, COD, or marriage. But the issue wasn't vital to me. I only expressed interest so as not to offend anyone.

M.D. remained vague, so I made to leave. He gave me another long/dog look. "You no want meeting my wife?" he said. Rather than answer, I offered to buy him and the whore a beer. I came back to the table with a couple of Heinekens.

"Hinkin!" said M.D. "He bring us Hinkin. Oh, you very big man. You are as boss." Oh cripes, I thought. I am as fool. Rule number thirty-two for getting by in Senegal: *never try to buy yourself out of a pain in the ass.* M.D., steadily tapping my leg, giving me a sinner's grin, said, "You like my sister?" He said this the way Millie Jackson would say, "You like my sweet thang, don't you, baby?" And for some reason still a mystery to me today, I said, "Yes-M.D.-I-really-like-your-sister-but-you-see-I-am-married." He looked at me as if I'd said, "I-am-in-Senegal," and without blinking, twitching, flinching, said, "You like my sister?"

"Yeah, she's very nice, but I'm married."

"I am marry too."

"Well, yeah right, so you understand what I'm trying to say to you." M.D. shrugged, sipped his beer, said, "You no like my sister I get 'nother sister." He turned toward the bar, waved, and a quarter of a minute later a woman in a green boubou billowed to our table. She was shorter than the first one, shorter on looks, and wasted. Wordlessly, she sat next to M.D.'s big sister, leaned toward the woman, buried her face between those indescribable breasts and nuzzled them for a long time. I mean a long time. M.D. told me it was supposed to make me horny. I don't believe it did.

Again I tried to shove off. Again I got the long/dog face and sat down. Not knowing what to do, I bought another round of beer, and tried to make small talk to Big Sister. I leaned toward her, and in my best Berlitz French, said, "*Votrage?*" She looked at me as if I'd spoken Hebrew, so I said, "*Votre nom?*" She sat blink-blink-blinking at me vacantly. I said, "Well, then do you give good skull?" She sat there. I sat there. I ordered four more beers and clammed up.

M.D. sucked down the last few clouds of foam from his beer glass and said, "You are very big man. You meet my wife now."

He took me straightaway to his little bantam-weight home in the village. His wife was indeed very ill. She lay in bed, dull-eyed and ugly as sin. A small, brown sack lay on its side next to the bed. Its contents—medicines of all sorts, pills, liquids, oils—were spilled onto the floor horn-of-plentylike. M.D. introduced me to his wife. I couldn't catch her name. Her smile looked delicate enough to be blown away by the wind stirred up by moth wings. She gave me her hand; it was hot, the skin dry, tough, and her grip strong. As I held her hand and smiled back at her, two little boys slid from behind a curtain separating the bedroom from another room. M.D. beckoned them, told them to take my hand. They did so. The both of them looked less than healthy. They stood grim-faced, penguinlike. The smaller of the two, a boy about five, whistled out his nose, wheezed and gurgled out his throat. I stood there wondering what dark, exotic disease I might be contracting.

M.D. offered me food. "Come and chop," he put it. I gravely told him I myself was very sick, married, and pressed for time, that I was homeward bound. He probably looked hurt here too, but as the room was lit only by a single candle, I was impervious to the crook and curve of his face in the semidarkness. He offered to walk me home. As much as I wanted to, I couldn't refuse his offer, as N'Gor is a maze, a tight sheepshank on the tip of the Cap Vert. The village is older than Western history. You could walk into N'Gor alone and pop out somewhere in the eighteenth century.

As we walked, it became apparent to me that M.D. was blitzed. We made slow progress as he had to stop to piss here and there. Moreover, he added to our mileage by sloshing side to side, or rearing two or three steps in order to pick up forward momentum. As we neared the hotel complex, he sidled up to me, and took my hand. "I have for you something I want give you," he said. I didn't know what to say, so I said, "Why?"

"Is because you are very big man. I give this no other man. You only. You—you are my brother, and very big man." The way he leaned against me, whispered deep in my ear, squeezed my hand to punctuate his words, made me want to slap the black off him. "You know juju?" he said. Here we go, I thought, and told him I'd heard of it, but knew very little about it. He licked his lips. "Juju," he said, "is very strong, very good. It make you protection. If a man he put you knife anywhere, anywhere on you is no cut or pain you."

"Oh yeah?" I said. I didn't know what else to say.

"Oh yes. Is true."

"And you want to give me this juju?"

"Is true. If man he put gun *or* knife for you is no pain." I wasn't the goddamnedest interested, moved, impressed. All I could think of was shucking the old boy and getting back to the soothing drabness of my bungalow. And as we neared the bungalow area, I turned to M.D. and thrust my hand at him, saying goodnight. He seemed shocked by this, said, "I want give you him this night." I stopped dead and eased my hand from his. "This very important," he said. "Too important. If a man gun he knife is no killing you. *Tu comprendre?*"

"Look, M.D., I'm very honored, you know, happy? that you've offered me your sister, and your juju and everything, but it's OK. I just want to be your friend.

"You are my friend, no?"

"You are my friend, yes, M.D., but I really don't need any juju."

We were near a hotel security guard when I said this, and because I'd spoken rather loudly, M.D. grabbed my arm and shushed me. "Is secret," he whispered. I was so flustered it took me nearly ten minutes to find my room. I must admit I was becoming intrigued. I ushered him into my room, offered him some gin and a seat.

After I listened to him rattle on about his sister's beauty, honesty, and breasts, the puissance of his juju and the bigness of me, Idi, Idrissa Ndaiye, my interpreter, stepped in without knocking. "Hey, Berd, What's happening?"

When I think about it, I've got to admit that *interpreter* is too fancy a word to attach to my friend Idi. We met on my fourth day in Senegal and immediately hit if off. And, since my French was virtually nonexistent, and my Wolof absolutely so, Idi usually would end up interpreting for me. I never paid him a dime, but because he loved speaking English, and perhaps because I could afford to buy and share with him things he loved but couldn't afford—Nigerian weed, American and British and Canadian cigarettes, good French bread, canned meats, and café au lait—I was pretty sure he felt fairly recompensed.

I liked him very much. His *moutoneux* head and skinny frame are all I truly miss about Senegal. I was so relieved to see him step through my door that night, it took me a moment to note M.D.'s transition from English to Wolof. When I did notice, I became suspicious that M.D. might be filling Idi's head with propaganda, telling my companion to be a brother and help M.D. skin me for a few dollars more. So I put up my mental dukes and suspended all belief in everything while Idi explained things to me. "No, no, no," said my interpreter, "the girl is really not a whore. She just wants to be like your girlfriend while you are here. She could live with you if you like, or you could just you-know-what with her whenever you want to." He wore a grin that would make Jack Kennedy look like a pyorrhea victim. A hero's grin. One of those grins journalists are fond of calling "winning smiles." I struggled to remain wary. "How much is it supposed to cost me?" I said.

"That's up to you, boy. How much do you give Lillian for making love?"

"I don't pay Lillian for sex. She's my wife, not my whore."

"Your wife?"

"Well, I told him that so he'd lay off, but it didn't make a dent."

"Well of course not." Idi frowned. "What does this mean to a Muslim who could have three or four wives? Look, wife, girlfriend—really this does not matter. My point is that even if you don't give her money, you give her things. You give her jewelry and clothes. You take her to dinner or buy her a little makeup."

"Be serious, Idi, I don't even know the woman."

"Who knows women?"

"Tell him I'll think about it." M.D. cocked an eyebrow at whatever Idi told him, which seemed to take longer than your standard, He'll give it some thought. M.D. nodded and said something to me. Idi turned to me, said, "He wants to know if you are still interest in the juju." I could read nothing in Idi's face. He looked Buddha-tranquil. "I don't know about the juju," I said. "I'm not sure what he means." Idi took a chair, folded his arms, crossed his legs and spoke to M.D. M.D. sipped his drink, set it on the nightstand, then spoke in Wolof. I listened to him as if his voice were music. I strained to hear something familiar in his voice, truthfulness or deceit, mockery or gravity. But it was useless, for I wasn't even certain whom he was addressing. He seemed to recede into the steamy night air. It was as if his voice came from stereo speakers, or wafted in through the windows. And then, slow and easy, like skillful counterpoint, came Idi's translation. It sent chills through me. Idi's English seeped into M.D.'s Wolof so perfectly that I couldn't tell whether his translation was for my benefit, or a sign of symbiosis between M.D. and himself.

"'This juju I want to give you was given me by my father more than twenty-five years ago. You must remember, my friend, that the juju cannot be bought or sold or it will lose the power in it. For the pass twenty-five years, I fear no man or creature. With this juju, I can walk anywhere with no fear or hesitation. As long as I wear it, nothing can penetrate my skin. Bullets cannot harm me; knives cannot harm me.

"'Many years ago I was a trader in Bamako. Perhaps you are not aware of all the dangers that wait inside Mali for a boy with stuff and money. There are many, my friend. So many that Death stands wherever your back is turn. Life has a tight, tight fist there, and not a week pass when there is no talk of some young, unprotec-teh fool found slaughter and free of all his worldly things, in the cold of early morning.

"'I was young, but not a fool. I carry this with me wherever I went.'" M.D. stood and lifted his boubou, grinned as if he were flashing. Looped round his flabby belly was a tubular leather belt, the ends of which were held together by a simple loop and a crude leather button. There was also a second button and a second loop, but these were left unfastened. M.D. dropped his head and looked at the belt, his bottom lip poking. He was sitting between me and the rickety lamp on the nightstand between the beds. His silhouette strikes me now as having looked like a shriveled Alfred Hitchcock's, although at the time no such simile came to me. I just wanted him to finish his story and go home. I was very uneasy.

He squinted down at me, said in English, "Mali is very dangerous," then sat down, dropped the hem of his boubou, and turned to Idi.

"'It was winter, and there I was, a young boy of twenty-five in the finest markets of Bamako with fine stuff to sell. I made, on my first day, a twenty-thousand CFA profit. There was nothing I could not sell. And I had everything. Did you want scissors?

American perfume? Right here, I got 'em right here. Watches, you say? *Rouge à lèvres,* you say? Come to Moustapha Diole.

"'My second day gave me another profit of twenty thousand CFA, and my next day brought me three times this much. By the end of one month only I was ready to return home. Imagine this. Here I was doing in one month what it usually take other to do in six.

"'On the night I was to leave there, I decide I should taste a little whiskey and a few women. I made my way to the night market not far from the airport to find those things. Before Independence, it was possible to find these markets. During the day, these markets appear to be simply regular markets, and as far as anybody knew, the day business was all they did. But at night, Berd, at night, *Wyyo!* many, many sweet and bad things could be bought in those places. Do you want a woman? No problem. Do you want a Russian rifle? *Voilà!* Human flesh, you say?'"

I was growing uncertain as to whose story this was. It seemed that Idi was on the verge of racing ahead of M.D. M.D. looked a bit baffled as Idi told me about the night markets. Even after Idi (evidently) explained to M.D. what he'd told me, I noted a shade of bewilderment sweep across M.D.'s face. He nodded once, twice, then asked Idi a question. "*Si, si,* No problem." M.D. resumed:

"'Yes, my friend. This was not a place for children, my friend. Here is a place where the spirit is too happy to leave from the body. Here is a place where money flies faster than airplanes?'" M.D. bugged his yellow eyes and thrust one bony finger toward the ceiling. He turned to me with the finger still stiff in the air and said, "Mali is very dangerous." He brought the finger down slow and easy as if drawing a curtain down on the English parenthetical. He turned to Idi.

"'I was in this place searching for what I wanted, when all of the sudden I heard a familiar voice call to me. I have the eyes of a village man. I can see coins at the bottom of the sea, but I saw no person this night. I turn around, and jump when I see to find myself face-to-face with a big and huge Mauritanian that I did business with some days before. Ah! he was a big, big, big. 'Hello, my friend,' he say. '*Asalaam aleikum,*' I say to him. 'You don't remember me, my good friend?,' say this *nar.* 'I certainly hope you do,' he say, 'because we made business together a few days ago only.' As he say this I slip my hand in my boubou, and close the second button of my belt. This I did, you see, to bring power to it. The *nar* continue speaking like this; 'You see my brother, I have change my mind about our bargain. I would like to return you these sunglasses. You see they are not the quality you promise.'

"'I don't know what you mean,' I say. 'I am arrive in Bamako yesterday only.'

"'You remember me and I remember you.'

"'Perhaps you met my brother,' I respond.

"'My money, nigger, give it to me.' Before I could move I saw the *nar*'s arm fall to me like a shadow. He hit me two hard times on my head with a knife. Before I could reach for my knife, he was on me again. He stab on my arm, head, and neck very crazily and angry. It was not until the fourth time he hit me that I realize that I was feeling no pain. Not one pain at all. The juju was working!

"'Suddenly, the *nar* stop his attack. His knife drop to the ground with a loud sound, and I hear him back away from me slowly. Then my hand found the handle of not my knife, but of my machete. I had it out at the same time he turn to run. I close my eyes and swing with the power of Mohammed almost. When I open my eyes I expect to see his big *nar* head rolling on the ground. Instead I was disappoint to see him run away like a baboon. I drop down to my hands and knees to feel for blood, but find only his right hand and most of his bottom lip.'"

Nice story, I thought. I looked at Idi for a good long while, trying to read his face. Nothing. The mastery he held over his face rivaled the Mona Lisa. It held balanced, soft, almost fuzzy, like one might hold a ball of light in the palm of one's hand. I wanted to throw something at him. M.D.'s eyes were yellow-yellow. They told me very little. They were as unreadable as Idi's eyes, but outlined with drunken nonchalance.

Then M.D. said something to Idi. "He wants to know," said Idi, "if you have a knife."

"What for?" I said, as if I'd just stumbled into the room. Idi looked at me as if I knew damned well what for, but nevertheless said, "He wants to prove the belt works."

"Is he serious?"

"I think."

"You mean he's going to stab himself?"

"Yes, I think."

"Tell him he doesn't have to. Tell him I believe him, but I'm just not interested."

"Doesn't matter, Berd. He wants to show you anyway."

"How do you know? Did you ask him?" I looked at M.D. He sat gravely nodding, bottom lip poking big as Texas, looking just as cool as cool can.

Now look. My little pocket knife is no kabar. The blade, at best, is a mere three or four inches long. It's sharp enough to pierce an orange with but slight pressure. With medium pressure, it's sharp enough to pierce the flesh. I often use it to punch new holes in my belts. I slipped the knife from my pocket, and, oddly enough, tossed it across the room to Idi, as if he were a member of the studio audience and M.D. the Amazing Kreskin. Idi cocked his head, opened the knife, got up, and handed the knife to M.D., who took the knife, uncovered his beer belly, fastened the belt's second button and peppered himself about two dozen times. He beckoned me, asking me to inspect his work. I did. There were about two dozen pin pricks on his belly, each holding the faintest droplets of blood. Otherwise, his stomach was fine. "*Aam,*" M.D. said, and handed me the knife. "Now you must stab him," said Idi.

"Tell him I believe him," I said.

"Won't do any good."

"Is true," M.D. said. "Is no pain you."

I looked from Idi's eyes to M.D.'s and back. Idi seemed rather bored. M.D. looked stoned, eager and somewhat supercilious. With one arm akimbo, bottom lip poking, he smacked himself on the belly, said, "Is strong. Very good." "I don't want to hurt him," I said to no one in particular. "I don't think you will," said Idi. I touched the knife point to the palm of my hand in order to gauge its sharpness. It seemed to me that one moderate poke would sink the blade an inch or two into the old man's stomach. I folded the blade. "Tell him to fuckin' forget it," I said. But Idi argued that it had become "a thing of honor," that I couldn't back out. "He say," Idi went on, "that you have brought him good luck. He say his wife has medicine because of you."

"That's because of the mark-up on the garbage I bought from him. It hasn't got a damned thing to do with luck. I was just too stupid to bargain with him." And then I went on about how I too was being honorable by pledging my belief in M.D.'s word. But Idi just stared at me as if I'd said something stupid. "You want me to tell him that?" said Idi. M.D. weaved and bobbed, daintily holding up the hem of his boubou. "No. Hell with it," I said, opening up the knife. I gently pushed the point into M.D.'s soft belly. I increased the pressure bit by bit. The knife depressed his stomach like a finger poke. I withdrew the knife, drew back and jabbed hard, then harder. I looked up and grinned at Idi. He was at the dresser fixing himself a drink. I shrugged and pounded M.D.'s stomach so hard the blade folded across my index finger and M.D. fell backward onto the bed.

Not a scratch. I turned toward Idi, who was now intently watching me. "Is true," I said.

So.

As Idi explained it, M.D., indeed, wanted to give me the juju, but this is the kind of giving he'd had in mind. I was to have named one price—any price—in exchange for the belt. All I had to do was name one price and the price would stick.

Haggling would negate the belt's power. And according to Idi, the only reason M.D. brought up the matter of money was because it was a ritual way of showing respect for the power of the juju, M.D., and M.D.'s poor dead dad. So there I was. I'd seen what M.D.'s miraculous belt could do, or more objectively, what his miraculous stomach could do, or what my eyes could not do, or whatever. I didn't know what to say. I vacillated between what was and what wasn't was.

Having the belt meant either going through the rest of my life essentially unafraid of another human being, or making a complete and very perforated ass of myself. I alternately envisioned myself single-handedly stopping crime in the United States, and winding up dead from self-inflicted wounds in my little Senegalese bungalow. I didn't know who how from nothing. And one matter, completely aside from the question of the belt's efficacy, was that of the money. If I'd offered him five dollars, think of the statement I'd have been making about M.D. and his father. On the other hand, what if I'd offered him fifty, or five hundred dollars? You just don't go around ready to hand out big simolea for things in which you don't believe. I wanted to say, Look, Idi, tell this yutz to go wax himself. He's a huckster. Tell him I'm a goddamn American and I don't believe in shit. I wanted to say, No, no, on second thought, I really don't believe this motherjumper works. Tell him to get me a goddamn gun I can poke in his eye. Then we'll see about this he-no-kill-no-pain hooey. I wanted to say, Get me back to Boston. I wanted to say, Help! Mr. Wizard, I don't wanna be an anthropologist no more! Instead I said, and quite soberly I might add, "Tell him," I said, "Tell him I'll think about it."

Anyway, Idi, who'd sat through the whole affair with his disengaged, beatific mug, told me next morning over café au lait and bread, that M.D. was more than likely trying to pull a fast one. He said the juju Moustapha Diole had offered me probably wasn't the one actually protecting him.

"He's not a stupid man," said Idi.

First I Look at the Purse

I'LL be honest with you. I didn't get my bone wet till I was seventeen or so. But I'll tell you one thing; I knew every way they was to make a hen unleash that mighty greenback. That's the important thing anyway. Least it was till I met Alicia. Any cat can get the boo boo if he beg an cry enough, but can't too many fellas get them bills.

You got to know how to do it. See, the average dude'll slide up to a hen and say, "Oooh . . . um . . . aah . . . mercy, sweetness, you sure is a fine thing." And half the time he end up standing in front of a double-barrel, "I-ain't-studying-you-Negro." She might grin at you and whatnot, but you put your funky hand near her and you be drawing back a nub. She'll shame you right down to your socks. My rap is what you might call peculiar. I'll ask a hen something like, "Say, sisterman, anybody ever tell you what's the surface temperature of Saturn?" And if she say no and smile, she yours. If she say yes, well, you best slide on back and go elsewhere.

The thing is you ain't got to know fact one about Saturn. You say this to make her stop dead in her tracks. She'll grin at you maybe, and think you silly, but I'll tell you something. A hen know it's a mature nigger who say something funny like that. She'll act all shy and whatnot and she yours.

Now, you take somebody like Michael Crawford. He was the only cat at Oakland High who even come close to a good rap, but he didn't know the first thing about getting a hen's money. Michael swore he was the baddest boy on platform shoes, but I know he was only two things: zero and nothing. He swore up and down couldn't nobody slick a hen like he could. But me, I didn't talk no stuff. I just did what I had to do and went about my business. Michael always be telling stories about how he and such and such a young lady was out behind the school doing the do from the end of track practice till late into the evening. Never shut up two seconds about it. But I showed him something.

Like last fall Michael and me was competing for the same hen, Alicia Patterson. This broad was not only a natural brick but she was stupid as a deacon (least we thought she was), and had beaucoup green. Her daddy was a CPA in Mill Valley. Something ungodly good happened to Alicia over summer vacation, 'cause last year that sister was sumo-fat and wore enough metal in her mouth to keep her head pointing permanent north. But niggers fell out all over the place when Alicia stepped through them halls in September.

I remember just how it was, too. Four or five of us was standing out in front of the school pitching quarters, when Frankie Smith nudge my arm and say, "Oooo?" I didn't pay no mind cause Frankie steady after them hens that look like Picasso's worst nightmare. But when Michael said "Oooooo?" I turnt around and like to fell out. After that everybody standing around saying, "Ooooo?" I caught holt of myself and slid on into the building. The worst thing you can do is let a hen know you acting a fool over her. She'll think you got something wrong with your glands and won't stop at nothing to torture you.

For a whole month I watched cats try Alicia and then fade like white folks' smiles when a group of loud-talking niggers hop on they bus. She steady be walking through them halls with that undulating behind of hers wearing out the seams of her skirt, them books held up to her titties, and all the coin jangling in her purse.

Finally, it was down to me and Michael. Michael'd walk up and down them halls grinning with them refrigerator-sized teeth when she so much as look in his direction, or trying to strike some bad pose like his name, Lance Romance, and he breaking her heart. His hair would be so waxed up the brothers took to calling him Kiwi. And he like to wear out his voice box with that "Ooooo, sisterman, you looking fine today . . . " You'd've thought he could've come up with a rap at least half as slick as his head.

I pretty much forgot about the broad myself. I kept busy with playing hoop and pitching quarters. I had to get motivated in school, too, cause my grades had fell from a 3.0 to a one something. Moms and Pops thought it was because of reefer and partying, but I always handled that stuff pretty good. What messed me up some was I'd cut classes and go to the city library and read up on religion and stuff. For some reason I got interested in anything religious. Except my folks' church, that is. All that hollering and testifying used to give me a natural headache.

I guess it had to do with all them folks who'd cut they hair and ring them bells and tambourines, wear yellow robes and talk about this cat Krishna. Everybody seemed to be getting religious then. Marvin Gaye was talking about Holy Holy and Mercy Mercy. Don't get me wrong. I wasn't about to be joining nobody's church or ashram or temple or ant farm or nothing. It's just that I never could stand not being hip to fads and stuff.

Like I said, I wasn't thinking much about Alicia for quite some time till I ran into Michael one day. He was toting a Bible. I just about died laughing at the nigger cause I knew the boy was a stone illiterate. Boy'd get eye strain reading traffic signs. So I asked him what the jig was with the Bible, and he told me he had found out Alicia's number. "The girl's religious, man."

"Who told you this?" I said.

"It's obvious, man. She never party. She never cuss. Ain't nobody got one finger . . . "

"So you think that book gonna get you in them legs?"

"Ain't but a matter of time before I do."

"What you gonna do when she take you to Bible study and

you start talking about the Book of Clyde or some shit? Man, you jivey."

So we got into this big showdown about who was the sorriest, and who was gonna make way with the hen first. I figured knowing what I knew about religion, and knowing from the get go that I could tell if a book was right side up or not and Michael couldn't, I made him a bet that I'd get to Alicia before he did.

"You on, fool," he said. And that was that.

One day I found myself sitting next to Alicia at a pep rally. Naturally, I didn't go to them things, but it was required. And while she's hooting and clapping all dainty-like, I say to her, "Say. Alicia, you got any idea how many moons you could fit inside Jupiter?"

"Say what?"

That's all they was to it. She had never seen nobody like me before. But I got to admit she was different from any babe I had ever run into. For one thing, she spent more money on me than anybody ever had before. She was fun. She'd take me to get some grub at McD's or some place and half the time I wouldn't even want to eat nothing. Turns out she wasn't no churchlady at all. She was what you call a Rosicrucian, which surprised me, cause she was a kissing fool. I'd never run into a hen that was so good who could kiss like she could. Girl could do some monster things with them lips.

I didn't know exactly what a Rosicrucian was, so I asked her a whole lot of questions about it. We'd take long walks in the evening and talk about all kinds of stuff. She turned me on to things like auras and magnetism. All this metaphysical stuff. Stuff I'd never heard of. Alicia could talk about ancient Egypt, Tibet, China, and make it sound like she'd been to all them places. Sometimes I couldn't listen to everything she said, cause, man, I'd be holding her hand and listening to her sweet voice, and my dick'd be harder than Chinese arithmetic. I couldn't never bring myself to lay down with her, though. She was too good. Now, I ain't saying I didn't take her money. I wasn't no punk. I just couldn't bring myself to take nothing else.

It was a trip. Freaky things would happen to me after them walks. I'd go home to sack out and have these weird dreams. It'd be like I was flying, man. I'd just about be done fell off to sleep and my whole body would start to tingle. Then, next thing you know, I'm flying out in space with all these tiny stars shooting through my body like little needles shooting through Jello.

Sometimes I'd go way out in space and fly into these rooms and halls that be like neon lights. Purple, orange, yellow, red, blue. They was as bright as the sun, but they didn't hurt my eyes. I'd run into these funny-looking people who'd fly by in spaceships that made Funkadelic's stage sets look like playground equipment. It wasn't like a nightmare. As a matter of fact, it was the most peaceful feeling I ever felt. Not like drugs. Not like sex. It was pure freedom. I could fly anywhere, as fast as my mind would let me.

Sometimes I'd just zoom around Oakland to check out my buddies' cribs. I'd see them sleeping or beating off, listening to the radio or like that. I seen Michael one time sitting on his back stoop smoking reefer and coughing his lungs out. I yelled down to him, "Yo, Kiwi, man. You ugly." But he was steady huffing and didn't hear me.

I'd wake up from them dreams and just lay in bed, thinking about Alicia all night till I went back to sleep. Took me a couple of weeks to ask her about what this whole deal was.

"Don't think about it," she said.

So I asked her if she had anything to do with it and she said, "No more than you do."

I said that wasn't no kind of answer. "Girl, you irritate me sometimes," I said.

And she kissed me on the cheek and said, "Then maybe I do have something to do with those dreams, Walter."

Mysterious broad.

Pretty soon I started to spend all my time with her. We'd go to concerts, movies. We'd go on picnics, which I had always felt was kind of sissy. But I had fun. And she'd pay for everything.

This one time her Pops took us down to San Jose where they got this place called Rosicrucian Park. I seen this Egyptian museum they got there. The place had real mummies, and shit made out of pure gold and jewels. And I just about freaked when we went to the planetarium. All them stars reminded me of them dreams she made me have. I learned a lot of facts and figures about stars and planets. Wrote em all down, too, just in case Alicia's well dried up on me someday. Man, we went all over that place. I never knew they had all that junk down in San J. All I ever thought I'd see down there was low riders which you can see just about anywhere if you want to. It was a stone strip.

I felt good with Alicia. I felt they wasn't nothing in the world wasn't possible with her. She made me think about things I had never thought about before. Like seeing the world, and going to college, quitting reefer (which I only thought about for about two minutes, but at least she made me think about it some), eating right, meditating.

I quit running with the boys after school, too. Not because Alicia said so, though. To be honest with you, they started to bore me some. I still ran with Frankie some, but A.J. and Michael simply got on my nerves. They didn't dig nothing spiritual, and they tended to think with the head of they dicks instead of the one under they doo rags. The only time I talked to Michael was when he'd tug on my sleeve to ask me if I'd trimmed Alicia or no. The cat got serious aggravating.

I was happy, sex or no. Alicia kept shelling out the coin and I kept her grinning.

One weekend I got Alicia to give me some coin so I could buy me some new tennis shoes. I had ruint my old ones playing on them courts out at Skyline High. I went out and bought me some pretty-ass Cons out at Freedman's and then run on home to get my ball. When I got home I got Alicia on the hook and told her to meet me over at Brett Hart Jr. They was the only courts with nets, and if you want to look good while hooping for a hen you got to have some net.

So I got down there a few minutes before I told her to be there so I'd have time to warm up. When I got there, though, Michael, Frankie, and A.J. was already there playing twenty-one and they called me over for a game of two-on-two. They jumped on me about where I'd been lately, and whycome I'd took to acting so sidicity. I shamed them into shutting up, though, when I asked them if they couldn't get along without me for three or four weeks.

Frankie and me took on the other two and whupped them 9–15. I told them I wanted to rest for awhile cause I was out of shape, but the truth was I didn't want to be too funky by the time Alicia got there. We sat down and talked about nothing for awhile, then A.J. asked me where I got my shoes. I told him I got them at Freedman's.

"He didn't ask you that," said Michael.

"Yeah," said A.J. "Where did you get the coin is what I want to know."

"Same place I always get it."

"Little Miss High-Yellow?" said A.J.

"Now what you think, fool? And that girl blacker than you."

"You jamming the broad?" said Michael.

"How many times you been in it?" A.J. said.

"How high can you count?" I said.

"You a lie," said Michael. "If you'd've got that stuff, you'd've been in my face for the money in a minute. You a damn lie, boy."

"Why would I take your little change when I can get money and leg from the same source?"

"You a goddamn lie," said Michael.

"Your mama," I said.

If Michael hadn't bounced that ball off my mug I would have whupped that high-gloss head of his, but he got the jump on me.

My nose started bleeding and my eyes was too full of tears to see right. He was up on his feet before I was and give me a couple of kicks to the side of my head. I fell back. He went upside my head with them bony knuckles and that was all they was to it. By the time my head stopped hissing all three of them was gone.

After a couple of minutes Alicia ran up to me. I was spitting blood and feeling stupid, and I just didn't feel like being humiliated. She asked me what happened.

"I done got run down by a bus, bitch. What it look like happened?" And then I leaped up, got in her face, and told her she wan't shit and to get the fuck away from me. She broke into some tears. I told her she better take her crying ass someplace else or I'd give her a reason to cry.

I felt bad about it, but what's done is done. It took awhile, but I started running with the boys again. I put the word out that Alicia and her family was Moonies and would invite folks over to they place and give them hoo-doo herbs to brainwash them. I told them that maybe she done slipped me a mickey or two cause I'd had strange dreams after every time I went out with her. By March or so she didn't have friend one in the whole school. Hen went completely to seed, too. Her hair'd be stone nap some days and she started putting on weight. Everybody thought it was because her hoo-doo had done wore off. Folks capped on her so hard she quit eating lunch in the cafeteria, quit going to ball games, dances, and whatnot. I figured it'd only be a little while before she quit going to school altogether.

Then a funny thing happened. It was near the end of school. Me and the boys was out in our usual place smoking and tossing quarters. Frankie nudged me on the arm and told me to turn around. I just about jumped back to the Stone Age when I seen Alicia coming straight to me like she just plain didn't know any better. She didn't say a word. Not one word. Hen walked up to me just as cool as cool can and stuck a note in my hand, turnt around and walked away. Everybody started hooting and yacking at her, asking her why didn't she turn me into a frog or spit up pea soup in my face or something. But Alicia kept steady walking like it wasn't nothing peculiar.

A.J. snatched the note from me but I collared him and told him I'd fire on him if he didn't turn it loose. I wasn't in no mood for play. The way Alicia had just walked up to me and stuck that note in my hand as casual and easy as she'd stick a dollar in it made me feel something seriously deep. I slipped the note in my pocket, collected my winnings, and split.

I didn't read the note right off. My palms was sweating, and I could not keep the usual cool. I got home. Moms asked me what was wrong. I asked her why, and she said I looked like I had done had a long talk with Death. I said to her I wasn't studying nobody's death.

"Well, why you come home so early?" she said.

I said school was out.

"Well, excuse me, Mr. Walter Ellis, but you usually running around with them hoodlum friends of yours till suppertime."

I said I wasn't studying no hoodlums.

"You sick?"

"No."

"You need money?"

"Mama, you know I ain't never broke."

"You been fighting?"

"Not today." I told her I was tired and just wanted to go lie down.

I went to my room, closed the door behind me, and stretched out on my bed. I stuck my hand in my pocket, pulled out the note, and laid it on my chest. I stared at it for a long time, thinking I might not read it at all. I just stared at the ceiling, the light fixture, the spider webs up in the corner. Maybe she want her money back, I thought. And I thought I just might give it to her, too.

I looked down at the piece of paper on my chest and watched

it rise and fall. It was like I was paralyzed. It went up and down. Up and down. Up . . . and . . . down. My eyes got real heavy. My body started to tingle. Maybe I will, I thought again. Next thing you know them tiny stars was tingling through my Jello body. I was deep in space.

Peaches

J.C. CROSSES the sun-faded carpet looking truculent and surly. He looks at me with his woman-get-out-my-seat face. His tail points straight up to the ceiling. He lets out with his most irate meow, stomps back and forth in front of me in that stiff-legged strut that drives me crazy. He always does this when I sit in "his" chair. "Looks like everybody's mad at me today," I say, crossing my arms and legs at the same time. Momma doesn't say a word so I know what's up with her. Daddy drops the paper to his lap, and sits up in his chair. Its old, arthritic wood creaks. "Ain't nobody mad, Baby Sister," he says, removing his glasses. "Ain't nobody disappointed, hurt, upset—'cept that little pea-brain cat of yours. Mystery to me why you even sit in that chair after he done rubbed all his hair off in it."

"Have you heard from Marc lately, Rita?" asks Momma, not looking up from her puzzle.

"Good Lord Almighty have I heard from him. Tuesday I got four letters. Four separate letters. In four separate envelopes."

"What's all this 'Lord Almighty' business, girl," says Daddy. "I ain't sending you to no twenty-thousand-dollar-a-year college to hear you talk like a imitation me. You gonna be a scientist. Let me hear my money's worth."

"Your money?" Momma says, "You mean Uncle Sam's money."

"I'll take his money too if it help put Baby Sis through school. I ain't proud."

"You ain't rich neither," Momma says, snapping a puzzle piece into place.

J.C. leaps up into my lap. His purring irritates me so I get up and move to the other side of the room.

"We got a postcard from him a couple of days before you got here, Rita," my mother says, still not looking up from the table. "Didn't say much though."

"Why didn't you tell me when I got home, Momma?"

"Moody as you was? No ma'am. I got better things to do than listen to you bawl from sunup to sundown. Anyway, we already talked about your plans before you got here. Now if I'd been bringing up his name all the time you might have thought I was trying to push you into sending him that . . . the—"

"How 'bout 'Dear John,' Lucille."

"James!"

"Daddy—"

"Well, that's the truth. I'm calling a spade a spade. Just like he did."

"James! Now I am not going to have you—"

"All right now, I'm just playing. But I don't care how much ass that boy kiss. And I don't care how long he stay in Africa to sensitivize hisself. Cain't no rich white boy call my child no nigger and—"

"Maybe not, but she grown, James. It's her life. Her decision. You and I got nothing to say whatsoever about what Rita decide. Now you promised me you'd leave the poor girl alone. Can't you see she upset as it is?" Momma snaps another piece into the puzzle, pushes her glasses up on her nose and looks up at Daddy. Daddy picks up the newspaper, crosses his legs, clears his throat. "You right," he grunts, then clears his throat again. "Yeah, you right. But if you ask me, you an apple, he an orange." I can tell from his eyes that he is staring at but not reading the paper. The room is as silent as the moon. Dust motes swim through the lamplight around Daddy's head. He looks hurt and I'd like to tell him he needn't be, because I myself am not hurting. I am numb. I don't know what to think or feel or do. I veer toward anger, then careen toward love, then roll toward regret and guilt. But as has been the case since the fight, I end up weightless and static like one of those motes around Daddy's head.

Daddy tosses the paper to the floor and in the silence it sounds like firecrackers. J.C. springs up from the chair and scoots under the couch. The room again falls silent, the brief flurry of sound and action is swallowed up like stones tossed into the ocean.

After awhile Daddy's chair squeaks and cracks. He inhales deep and slow, then slips on his glasses. "I believe," he says, "I could use a little help outside picking some peaches for old Mrs. Li's sweet and sour sauce. She says she gonna make some extry for you to take back to school with you. Come on."

The fog has not yet lifted, but the air feels dryer than usual. Mr. Givens's dog yaps at us from behind the gray cedar fence. In the thirteen years my parents and I and my two sisters have lived here, I've never seen the old dog and I don't know its name. Each evening, when chastising the dog, when telling it to shut up, when calling it in, Mr. Givens calls it, "Git-yer-dumb-ass-outta-that-garden, Shut-the-hell-up-ya-stupid-mutt, and Giddin-here-ya-damn-dog." As far as I can tell the dog seldom obeys. In the evenings Mr. Givens can often be heard bellowing, "OK, then don't eat, ya stupid!"

When the dog has barked long enough, my father picks up the usual peach pit, zings it in the area of Mr. Givens's garden, and finally we hear: "How many times I gotta tell ya to keep yer dumb ass outta that garden?" Silence. My father and I are alone in the backyard which is redolent with the smell of peaches, the sight of peaches. We feel peach pits beneath our feet.

"Grab that raggedy-looking box over next to the fence, Baby Sis," Daddy says. "Half them bushel baskets old Givens give me cain't hold air."

"This one?"

"Um hmm."

"Do we need a stepladder?"

"Well, they should be plenty of good ones on the ground. And if we shake us a branch or two we won't need a ladder." He kneels and begins sorting peaches, asks me a few questions about how school is going. I answer him in monosyllables, hoping the conversation won't drift toward anything that will upset us both. The afternoon air becomes cool all of a sudden. Goosebumps erupt on my arms and neck. "Daddy, I'll be right back," I say, "I need a jacket."

In my room I stand before the closet door, looking at my reflection in the full-length mirror. I look at myself, forgetting for several moments why I have come into the room. There I stand in baggy white pants and what Marcus calls my "favorite Dinty Moore shirt." He never told me he disliked the way I dress, but when I was clad in my flannels and baggies his eyes often glanced around—toward the bookshelf, "Hey, a new one by Mishima?" or my stereo, "Let's listen to some Marvin Gaye," or the Dali prints, "When did you say that one was painted?" He, like most men, wants to see women dress in anything tight enough to keep the blood static. He always told me he wasn't particularly a breast man, or a leg man—"I'm not an anything man," he'd say. "I'm an everything man. Legs, ass, brains, conscience." But he only seemed to tell me that kind of thing when I was wearing flannels and baggies.

"What does he see in me?" I think as I peruse the frizzy, uncombable black hair, the burdensome breasts, the face that he insisted no guy on campus could forget, the legs he insisted are not birdlike. "And look at my legs," he'd say, indicating with both hands, "They look like a couple of Venus number twos." He told me never to change a thing about myself. "I'm the one who needs to change," he'd say. And I'd tell him, in the beginning, he didn't need to change. That he was fine the way he was. But he would always sneer, "Simmons, you don't know the half of it." He kept saying things like that, becoming more strident, histrionic, and distant. "I'm no goddamned good," he'd say over and over. And soon enough, I began to feel as though his kisses were trying to smother something, that the walls of his apartment enfolded secret passages and chambers, that his conversation, numinous and trivial, full of New Age jargon, spoke around rather than of something. There was always something fleeting about him. Something just out the corner of my eye, something just out of reach. I imagined that an invisible incubus paced between us when we were together, thumbing its invisible nose at us, flipping us the invisible finger. I felt its presence so acutely, sometimes, that I could almost see it burst forth in hyperactive, muscled flesh. Sometimes it made me fear him. Sometimes I think it made me love him more.

The more I loved him, the less I understood him, the farther I slipped from him. And when he started punching walls, calling me at two in the morning to apologize for no reason at all, threatening to slash his wrists every time I told him I was busy, I sensed how ripe he was for procreation.

"You never have time anymore, Rita. What's the matter, you mad at me?"

"Why should I be mad at you? I'm mad at me. I've got to really get going on my thesis."

"I know, I understand. I just want to see you. Why are you hiding from me all of a sudden?"

I'd say nothing.

"What's wrong, Rita? I just want to see you for one hour."

"Marc, I just haven't got the time."

He never let up. He'd set his heels and push. And push.

"Is it something I said to you? Is it my beliefs? When we first met you always said I was too rarified for you. You said I strut around 'up there' acting fey while you're 'down here' accepting life for what it is. 'Fey,' you said. Jesus Christ, Rita, I got no problem with your science. Why can't you give me what's mine?"

"I know, Marc. I know. I should. I do. It's got nothing to do with your beliefs. Really. I'm just preoccupied. I've got two midterms tomorrow. I've got that lousy seminar. We can talk about this tomorrow, at dinner."

And push.

"It's because you think I got no soul or some crap like that, isn't it? I just can't give you what a black guy can give you, right? That's what you think, isn't it? Well if it is, Rita, then you're wrong. It's all an illusion. It's maya. If anything, I can give you more because my world is so different from yours."

"Marc, there's only this world—"

"Look, Rita, I've been through this before. I've had relationships with Black women and Hispanic women, and Asian women. You can tell me. I think I'd understand. You probably think I don't take you seriously. You think I'm just using you."

He'd ask me if it was his disapproving family, his derisive friends, his age, his intellect, or that he was an undergraduate English major and I was a semester away from a master's degree in chemistry. It often left us very little to talk about at dinner. He's ask if his beard looked silly, or if he dressed poorly, or if my family really hadn't liked him but had simply been Oscarwinning polite, or if he was too easily depressed, irascible, antisocial, untruthful, or was I sure-really-sure "it's not because I'm white?" I'd always say no.

I'd say no because it was easy to say no. Easier than unleashing untenable fears, easier, after awhile, than holding him close, feeling his diffuse heat. He'd push, and it was if he'd started pushing too deeply inside himself, rummaging and scraping, uncovering things that I'm not sure were ever there. "What's wrong with me?" he'd demand. "Tell me. Just tell me something. Do you still love me? Do I offend you in some way?" I couldn't tell him. I knew I'd just have to wait, then I'd see, he'd know. I'd tried to tell him once or twice, but everything would lock up inside me when I'd try to explain. And then it finally just slid out from him, loud and ugly. The word. The beast-incubus word, the inevitable issue of the "yin-yan" relationship.

His phrase, "yin-yan relationship." Had I drawn it from him, headfirst screaming, kicking into the world? Or did he plant it in me, water it with his tears, incubate it in the heat of my womblike reticence? I don't know.

All I could say that night was, "That, Marc. That's just what I was afraid of. Wasn't but a matter of time, was it?"

How would things have gone if I had just told him of my fears and talked it out with him? I never did because to do so would have implied that he had transcended nothing. I flat would have been calling him a liar, or blind. And he was neither. He had transcended something, somehow. Or what if I had just buried myself in his auburn beard, his ginseng breath, the bend and curve of his body, and listened to his nonsense about the Ghosts of Lemuria, the Light of Atlantis, the Race of Tan just for the sake of hearing his voice. His voice was so nice to listen to, a little raspy, a little flutelike. Sometimes it seemed he told his stories in song. Sweet nonsense. And when I actually heard him say the word I was so sure he would eventually say, I was shocked. Shocked both because it always shocks you when someone calls you nigger and because the word fell from his mouth so awkwardly—as if he had never heard it before, said it before, imagined saying it before.

So he bought a ticket to Liberia. I didn't know what to feel. He told me he wouldn't come back till he knew, till he really, really understood what blackness was. I didn't know what to say. He hugged me, kissed me longer than I could stand, said goodbye, promised he'd change, we'd get it straight, he'd return reborn, we'd marry and raise fat, tan, unrarified babies. He got on the plane. He called me from Denver. He called me from New York. He called me from Dakar. He called me from Monrovia. I got his first letter in two weeks. By six weeks I'd received eight more. In three months over forty letters. Bombarded by missives of love, the seed of self-discovery. They came daily, weekly. Tidings of hope, love, joy. Peace Profound. Images of beautiful babies, beautiful ocean, sleek, cat-black men, women in rich Day-Glo rags. The taste of this. The smell of that. The size, shape, volume of his ever-expanding, ever-pregnant African love. But I just didn't. His seed fell on unsettled dust, a haze of motes never coming to rest.

"It won't lie still," I say aloud, suddenly remembering why I've come up to my room. I grab something warm-looking and bluish, then run back outside.

I stand on the stoop and watch Daddy kneeling in the grass, peach in hand. He sniffs, squeezes, removes his glasses and inspects it, then tosses it aside. His face is grave, almost sullen. I cross the yard and kneel beside him, trying to imitate the way he inspects the peaches, but I'm not really sure what he's looking for.

I've always loved the way my father throws himself into the task at hand. Whether it be selecting peaches for Mrs. Li's sauce, adjusting a bicycle seat, or expounding to three enraptured daughters at the dinner table just what it is that makes a grocery clerk's job so much more dangerous than a San Francisco cop's, there is no one I know with the intensity, the undivided surrender to the action, the moment.

While we sort through hard, woody peaches and soft, muddy peaches, peaches bruised and scarred, peaches clear-complected, he tells me the secret of Mrs. Li's sauce: "She take a whisk broom to J.C.'s chair and use all them cat hairs and cookie crumbs y'all leave in it." And he hints at the secret secret to his peach cobbler, which he says he extracted, through torture, from a Japanese POW. "If I told you, you wouldn't eat it." He tells me it once rained peaches in San Francisco when I was "just a baby, and couldn't possibly remember." And that old Moses told God that no way on earth would he sign those "commandoes or commandants, or whatever you call em, till you take peaches off the list." He tells me he never would have looked twice at Momma had she never stuffed peaches under her sweater back in '47, that peaches, at one time, contained an explosive substance instead of sugar, and the last recorded use of the exploding peach was in the Boer War. "That was before your time," he is quick to add. He tells me about the Peach Bowl of 1968 (LSU won because they ate more peaches. "Well, why you think they call it Peach Bowl?").

"Paul Robeson couldn't sing note one 'less he had two, three quarts of peach wine in him," he says. And he tells me about all the peachy-keen people he had ever known (me, Juanita, and Theresa May, "and sometimes that hard-head mother of yours"). He tells me how Big Daddy used to push his cart around the streets of Alabaster, Alabama, hollering, "Waaaatermelon? Strawberries and Peeeeachez! Cold, sweet Peeeeachez!" Peaches and cream, peach ice cream, peacherinoes and peacherines, peach yogurt, peach popsicles, peach lipstick, peach pie, jam, and jelly. "Cold, sweet peeeeachez!"

The box is full of what he assures me are the finest peaches that soil could possibly produce. I offer him a peach from the brimming box; he frowns and says, "Shooot, naw, Baby Sister, I cain't eat them things." We laugh for a long time, leaning away from each other, folding toward each other, like jazz dancers. And then I start to cry. I cry so hard I can scarcely breathe. Daddy holds me, saying nothing. He doesn't even try to shush me, just holds me till I stop. Then he reaches in the box, takes out a peach, examines it, sniffs it, throws it aside. He takes another one and does the same thing. Then another, and another, and another, and another.

Finally, he turns the whole box over. Peaches tumble across the lawn. He inspects every last one. His long fingers caress each, every one. His nose and eye, inspecting, seed-deep, each, every one. And then he finds what he is looking for. It is very large, the color of a sunrise, flows into a sunset, flows into the color of Mrs. Li's blush. He rubs it on his sleeve, holds it out to me in the palm of his hand. I wipe my nose with a finger, regard the peach for a long, long time. Till Daddy's arm trembles a bit. "Naw," I say, "I can't eat em." He drops the fruit and it cracks on the green grass. He takes my hand, and we walk inside.

Who Big Bob?

THE whole five of us picked that cotton from sunrise to sunset. It was hard work and cut our arms and hands up something fierce. Snakes was every place you put your feets. Them bales busted our nuts. Not to mention that it got to be hot enough to blister backs as black as river mud. And ol Shockley got hot too. He your typical colored farmer. Nasty. Hard as a rock. Son of a bitch spent all day spitting tobacco, knuckles on his hips, and talking about "I'ma get rid a four a you niggers when that new gin get in. Ain't a one of you worth a hot gotdamn." He been waiting for that gin since I got here in thirty-one. But still it got on everybody's nerves. Kind of made us extry tired. That's why us five got together Saturday evening after supper. We played cards, smoked some of Shockley's cigars Walter'd done snatched, drank liquor, and talked trash way past midnight. Calvin played that mean guitar. Merlie and Walter brung the tightest shine that ever crossed my lips. We was all higher than a ribbon snake up a plum tree. Crickets was cricking. Frogs was frogifying. Moon was like a big, white belly.

Then Professor Longwind, who tell a story like nobody's bidness, waited till we was all full, slow and glowing, and said: "Sheeit. Ya'll think it was hot today? Let me tell ya'll about when I was bounty hunting in Texas back in ninety-eight. Come to find myself in a roody-poot little town name of Quemado, along the Rio Grande. Now it was July, and you wanna know hot? Boy, you ain't seen hot till you step into Quemado, Texas, in mid-July. Oooo Lawd, Lawd, Lawd. It was a hundred and seventeen, eighteen, twenty-something degrees out there if it was a one. The sun was hot enough to boil the Rio Grande and steam cook the red beans growing along the banks. So I wasn't the least bit surprised to find all the streets empty when I got in round half past one in the afternoon. Only a broke-dick fool be out on a day like that one. The sun up there grinning like Shockley when the heat be cooking his brain too deep, tall grass, growin out of sidewalks, dead as broom straw, windows melting like ice, birds roasting up in trees like it was Christmas day.

"Naturally, I wanted something cold to drink, so I looked up and down the street for a bar. I was tired cause I had done rode seventy-five miles that day looking for a killing fool by the name of Wallace A. Faubus Jr., who had done kilt hisself about twenty-three men on account he had a very bad attitude about who he wanna share a sidewalk with. Now, Quemado was just the right kind of town for Faubus to hide in cause it was one of them places that wouldn't know him from President McKinley. They didn't have no newspaper, and people was too poor and busy to pay much mind to things that was going on up in northeast Texas where I was from.

"Anyhow, my throat was dry and I was real thirsty. After I searched for about five minutes, the sun started to crawl up under my conk cover and my eyes started doing all kind of peculiar which-a-ways. I went into a barbershop quick as I could, but it didn't seem to be a soul in the place. 'Yo now,' I said. 'Anybody here?' I stepped up a little further into the place. Didn't get no answer. 'Yo now,' I said again. No answer. I turnt back to the door ready to head out. All of a sudden, I heard a loud noise which said, 'Scroo-oo-oot!' the way furniture sound when you pull it cross a floor. I whipped back around with my guns drawn. I wasn't scared. Nothing scared me. I been in many wars as a young man, and guns, bullets, bombs, wild hounds, and loud noises don't scare me. I only figured somebody might be in trouble and might need my help. I run to the back of the shop and opened the door. Before I could take one step into the room, somebody hollered and a shotgun said, 'Boo-looo!' I jumped down to the floor and stayed down there for a minute. No sir, I was not scared.

"Then, somebody said. 'Mister? Mister? You OK?'

"'I ain't hurt,' I said, 'Why, you shooting at me?'

"I got up off the floor, figuring the fella wasn't gonna shoot no more since he done ast me was I OK. 'Name's Longwind. Bounty hunter,' I said, 'and less your name Faubus you got no need to shoot me.'

"'Didn't mean to,' the voice said back. 'Thought you was Big Bob.'

"'Who Big Bob?'

"I looked around, guns still drawed. Didn't see no one. Only saw two old barber chairs and some big crates. 'Where you at?' I said. 'Come on out. I ain't gonna hurt you.' Put my guns away. Out from behind one a the barber chairs come this scrawny, watermelon head barber, with glasses and no hair. 'Sheeit,' I said. The barber just stood there with the gun in his hands, staring at me with his gasper goo eyes. Then, he said, 'I'm real sorry, sir. Like I said, I thought you was Big Bob.'

"'And like I done said, who Big Bob?'

"The man put the gun down. 'Well, sir,' he said, 'he the biggest, craziest, meanest, toughest, angriest, ugliest hombre in the entire state of Texas. He dangerous. He done kilt two-hundred-twenty-two men, women, children, horses, and what-not. When it get hot like this he come up from Morelas way where he live. Folks say that whenever the weather get up above a hundred and two Big Bob ain't fit to play with a string of spools. He kill a slew a people every time he come to town so everybody run and hide when the word get out he heading this way.

"'You look like a intelligent man, Mr. Longwind, you ought to be doing just the same. Big Bob don't like nobody, see. He come into town this time every year, go to the bar and drink up every drop of liquor in town. Then, after he all drunkity wild, he break everything he see: trees, wagons, chi'ren, dogs. . . . In a word or two, Mr. Longwind, he dangerous. DANGEROUS!'

"While he was talking his eyes got bigger and bigger, till they like to bust out the sockets. He tol me about the people Big Bob done kilt. He tol me how strong this Big Bob was. Said the big bastard destroyed the entire town of Spofford by smacking his head upside buildings. 'Dangerous,' he said again and again. Then I looked at the boy and simply grinned. I said, 'Sheeit. I ain't a-scared of nothing.'

"'Don't matter. Big Bob'll bust you in two just the same.'

"'I'm not afraid. I was in many wars as a younger man, and guns, bullets, bombs, wild dogs, and big men don't scare me. I done traveled all over this world and I seen many things. Naw, sir, I ain't studying your Big Bob. I'm here on bidness, and ain't leaving till bidness is done. Now. Looky here. It's hot as a three-legged calico queen. Where the bar at?'

"The little barber didn't said nothing.

"'Where the bar at, I said.'

"'You crazy, Mr. Longwind.'

"I pulled out a pistol. The one on my lef side, to be exact.

"'I ain't gone ast you again, boy.'

"'Well, it's your own neck I guess, Longwind. Out the door and to your lef. Cain't miss it.'

"I put my horse in the livery stable, and watered him down best I could. I walked to the bar. The buildings was smoking like fact'ries. I figured it wouldn't be too long before they'd pop into flames. Got to the bar in no time. Course it was empty except for the bartender. He was very surprised to see me there and tol me about Big Bob. When he finished flapping his soup coolers I grinned and said like this: 'Sheeit! I ain't afraid of nothing. I fought in many wars as a younger man, and guns, bullets, bombs, wild hounds, big men, nor big *crazy* men don't scare me. I done traveled all over this world and seen many things. Naw, sir, I ain't studying your Big Bob. I'm here on bidness and ain't leaving till bidness done. Now. Looky here. It's hot as a horn toad's three-bean fart out there. Gimme some tonsil varnish and make it snappy.'

"I had three, four whiskies, and ast the bar-dog up and down about Faubus, but he didn't know nothing. I was feeling good anyway. The bar-dog kep telling me stuff about Big Bob and I be steady laughing in his face. Then I heard this noise that said, 'Shtoom! Shtoom! Shtoom!' Footsteps. 'Shtoom! Shtoom! Shtoom!' Six-foot nine, give or take a inch. 'Shtoom! Shtoom! Shtoom!' Four, five-hundred pounds. 'Shtoom! Shtoom! Shtoom!' Big, big, big man coming. I knew that much. 'Run, mister, run,' the bar-dog said. But I just chuckled.

"Then the hugest, pug ugliest man I ever seen, come through the doors. I didn't said he opened the doors. He walked *through* the doors. Doors broke into a million tiny pieces. The man walked slow up to the bar. Looked like he was made up of nothing but muscle, bone, and bullwhip. Six foot, eight-and-a-half-inches tall. He had just one eye, all red and nasty looking. He had a big black beard that looked like a bird nest, and kep rubbing it with the back of one shovel-size hand. He had a enormous buck knife in his belt that was the size of my arm. I looked up at his big, ugly face. Great googly-moogly, the boy was uglyyyyy! 'How do?' I said, just as calm as I please. He looked down at me with that one red eye and didn't said nothing back. He just picked up a whiskey bottle and bit off the top, sucked down all the booze in about two seconds, then ate the whole bottle, chewing it real slow. Then he grabbed a handful of pretzels, grinded em into a fine powder and sprinkled em into his mouth like salt. After that, he cleaned his teeth with his big knife, slapped down six bits, turned and began strutting out the door. 'Hold up a minute,' I said. I looked over to the bar-dog and winked. Then I said to the big fella, 'It's hot as Lucifer's lunch out there, son. You ain't gonna stop at one drink, is you?'

"He stopped, turnt round to me real slow. Then he said,

'That's right. I got to hurry. Big Bob coming and I gots to get on out of town.' He turnt back around to the door again.

"'Hold on, bud,' I said. 'Name's Longwind. Bounty hunter. I been in many wars. You wants comp'ny?'"

Professor Longwind scratched his neck and grinned. "That about as hot as things can get," he said. Merlie was dead sleep. But Walter, Calvin and me, we was crying, laughing.

Uncle Moustapha's Eclipse

IDI, my very best friend here in Senegal, was suffering from a very strange eye malady. He didn't know precisely what had caused his usually quick, pebble eyes to swell, yellow, tear, and itch so. He'd gone to both doctors and *marabous* and they didn't know either. "All that I can say," said Idi, "is that my eye sickness remind me very much of my Uncle Moustapha's eye sickness." And at that he proceeded to tell me the story of his Uncle Moustapha M'Baye's eye "sickness":

"This was a long, long time ago, Marcus. Before I even was born. My uncle live in a small, small village along the Gambian river near to Bassi Santa Su, call Sakaam. It is too, too hot there. You would not believe it, my friend. The sunshine is so heavy there that a man can reach his hand into the hot air and squeeze the sunshine like wet clay. The mosquito there can only walk and the baboons move like old men, in Sakaam.

"It was there my Uncle Moustapha live and work with his three wives and seven children. He, it is say, was the finest peanut farmer in his whole village. He hardly never had a bad crop. When even there was too much rain, his crop was fair, and other farmers' much worse. And when the rains were thin, Uncle Moustapha always have plenty of rice for he save from the good years. This mean he was a very careful man. He was a hard worker, and very lucky. He had strong juju and was also a good Muslim.

"His only problem in life was that always, always he think about Death. He always think about Death most deeply on the night before his birthday. Now, you must understand, Marcus, that even when I was born thirty years ago, people did not know their birthdays. But Uncle Moustapha was very fond of many things in white culture. He like chocolate and watches, books and French bread. He like birthdays too, because my father tell me, he was a proud man and like the idea of having a personal day of celebration. So he begin keeping a birthday from the day his seventh child was born. He begin at the age of forty, and every year for twenty years, he keep the day of June seven as his birthday. This only add to his worry, for as we say here, Marcus, Death is birth and birth is Death.

"So on the eve night of his sixtieth birthday, he think about his death and he could not sleep. He lay in his hot room and no sound came to his ears. He wait with a numb heart for Death to enter any minute. He focus on nothing but the door, knowing that his final moments were upon him. He expect that soon, soon, a long, white hand would push the door open with no sound; that Death's face would be reveal to him and that he would be taken. He was not really afraid to die. Only he was very worry that his lazy brothers would not take good care of his wives and children. 'The moment I see this door open,' he say, 'I shall light a cigarette and smile at the old fool.' He feel for his cigarette and his matches. Upon coming into contact with both, he let his hand rest on them and say in a loud voice, 'How do you do, Death? Do you care for a smoke? No, no we have time, you and I; have one . . . yes, yes, of course. I have plenty left. Have one with me . . . indeed, master, sit anywhere. . . . So how are you? Been busy lately?' This make him laugh, you see, but only for a brief moment. He choke back his laughter when he notice that he cause his wife to wake. 'Why do you wake me?' she say.

"'I wait for Death,' he say, 'as always. My birthday is tomorrow, you remember.'

"'Ah, you crazy man,' my Auntie say. 'These whiteman ways make you too, too silly. To talk and laugh with yourself is madness. Madness, you hear? If you have no birthday, you have no fear of Death.'

"'I do not have . . .'

"'First it is chocolate which make you sick always. Then it is watch which make your wrist turn green. Then it is birthday which make you fear Death and ignore the courage that Allah give you. Then it is foolishness about sun . . .'

"'It is eclipse, you old 'ooman. Eclipse. And it is true. There are a thousand of white men in Bassi Santa Su who wait for it. They say the sun shall disappear and I believe them. It will be tomorrow on my birthday. You shall see.'

"'Dugga doff tropp,' she say, which mean my Uncle Mousse was a very crazy man. Auntie Fatima was my uncle's favorite wife, but not because she was always sweet to him, but because she always tell him the truth. His other wives always would smile at all his curious doings and hold out their hands for the *xallis.* Fatima love him the most, and and she did not care for a man with a lot of *xallis.* She say when he was first having birthdays she did not mind much. She used to even sit up with him each night before his birthday and humor him. But through the many years, as you say, Marcus, no dice. It make her angry.

"So she say, 'Dugga doff tropp,' to him and turn away to sleep. Uncle Moustapha only shrug, get up from bed and cross the room to where his clothes were. He reach into the pocket of his boubou and remove his watch. It was some minutes after midnight. He lay the watch on the floor and then say his prayers, thanking Allah with all his heart.

"'Get up, old man' say Auntie Fatima. 'Get up, I say.' It was morning. Uncle Moustapha open his eyes, but seem to see nothing as he always did in the mornings. His old bones were sore. He look about himself with his blind eyes and say, 'Fatima, it is dark, yet. Why do you wake me?' Auntie Fatima look at him and say, '*Wyyo!* Did you not ask me to wake you at cock-crow? It is you who ask me to do this so that you may see this Sun foolishness.'

"'Where did I put my watch?'

"'I do not know where is this watch,' say Auntie and she leave the room.

"Uncle Moustapha leap from his bed and find his watch. It was six o'clock and some minutes in the morning. There was still plenty of time for him to get to Bassi Santa Su before the eclipse. He wash his body, had a breakfast of bread and bitter black coffee, and put on his best boubou. 'Fati!' he say. Autie Fatima return to the bedroom. 'Fatima,' he say, 'I will take my lunch in town today.'

"'There is someone to see you, Mousse,' say Auntie.

"'Why did you say nothing to me?'

"'He came only this moment.'

"'Who is this who comes here?' say my uncle, very angry. You see, he want no one to interfere with his trip to town on this most important day. 'It is a white man' my Auntie say, 'with many strange machines.'

"'The name is Madison,' say the white man. And it seem he was a scientist interest in renting some of Uncle Moustapha's land to set up his machines and telescopes on. Uncle Mousse's land is green, green and beautiful as heaven. It is call the jewel of Sakaam, and I would not be surprise if Madison the white man want to stay at there because of its beauty, but he say instead that it was the perfect scientific place for him to view the eclipse because of all these scientific reasons. 'How much may I give you, Mr. M'Baye?' say Madison. And he reach to his pocket for some money. Uncle Moustapha stop the white man's hand and say, 'Wait, wait, wait! I want no money from you.' This shock Madison to make his green eyes stick out and his face turn red, red.

"'But your land is perfect,' he say. 'I need it. I will pay you any price.' Uncle Moutapha say no. This make Madison even more shock for he have never seen a black man refuse money, you see. 'But I do not want this money,' say Uncle Mousse. 'Please allow kindly, Mr. Madison, for me to view the eclipse with your machines.' Uncle Moustapha explain, that because it was his birthday, he must be allow to see this very special gift from Allah. Madison only shake my uncle's hand and smile a big, big smile.

"Time move slow, slow for the two men. The eclipse begin at eight o'clock and some minutes in the morning, and all the land and sky change to a mysterious, curious haze. Like a pearl. Many people stay in their homes because this cloudless sky was becoming darker and darker. Uncle Mousse was singing and dancing inside himself because it was his personal day and a very strange important thing was happening. But like a true Wolof man, he was quiet and serious outside. He help Madison the white man assemble his equipment as Madison explain to him many things about telescopes, eclipses, etcetera. The sky grew darker. It became empty of birds and the land was quiet and golden green.

"Every few moments Uncle Mousse would turn his eyes up to the sky of haze to look at the Sun, but when Madison one time saw this, he say, 'Mr. M'Baye, you must not look at the Sun. It is too dangerous. One could go blind from such a thing.' Uncle Moustapha say nothing, but he did as Madison say.

"When the machinery was prepare, my uncle and the white man take turns viewing the sun. Uncle Moustapha was astonish. Never did he see something like this in his life. Finally, the sky was as dark as early evening. 'Happy birthday, Mr. M'Baye,' say Mr. Madison. My uncle was overjoy. This was his gift from Allah, a present from his ancestors. He shake Madison's hand and walk away very quickly to his home with the memory of the orange-black moonsun deep in his mind. 'Fati,' he yell, 'Fati! You must come go with me to our baobab tree.' This shock and surprise Auntie because Uncle Mousse never had interest in baobab tree or in the spirits of the old ones, though he respect them.

"So, anyway, he take Auntie Fatima and tell her all he saw and all what Madison had say him. They walk in the semidark to the great baobab tree of the M'Baye family. The baobab tree, as you must know, Marcus, is the great and huge upside-down tree in which, it is say, live the spirits of the village. The tree that belong to Sakaam (perhap you have seen it when we were there together) sits on the great knoll on the edge of the village very close to the river. It stands alone there; more alone than any tree or shrub or twig in the entire environs. The most remarkable thing about this baobab is the curious way it bows to the east. It resembles a faithful servant of Allah.

"Uncle move as if he were pull to the tree. He ran the last few meters, pulling Auntie along with him. Then he let go of her hand and threw himself at the base of the tree. He say a silent prayer to himself and with his hands, grasp the enormous roots. Auntie Fati say it is as if the very touch of the tree make him feel a sudden power of the spirit, and cleaning of his heart and mind. He seem to empty his heart on the red soil under him as he begin to sing the ancient song of our ancestors.

> Oh fathers. Oh Mother
> Welcome to our hearts
> You will bring us comfort
> At the setting of the Sun.

"Of course, this strange behavior in my uncle did not too much surprise my Auntie Fatima because, as I say, she love him so much. She fall to her knees and say a prayer too. Then she rise when Uncle Moustapha rise and kiss him and say to him in English, 'Fine birthday to you, crazy old man.'

"'Ahh and then, Marcus, my uncle's senses at this moment became strongly, powerfully alive. His ears heard like a bat. He smelt the river and the earth and the rustling grass, the sweet, hot air. The smells about him were as strong as the smells of the ocean or a steaming bowl of *tjebugin.* His eyes took in everything—everything. He view each individual stock of yellow-green grass, every twig, every pebble that sat on the ground. The twigs had made the earth look like to be an enormous patchwork boubou. The soft air touch him delicately as a smile. He turn slowly around—seeing, smelling, hearing everything no matter how small, small or subtle or obscure. And with not one moment of hesitation, he lift his face to the sky and stare directly into the eclipse with his both eyes wide open. He stand staring, unblinking, unflinching.

"He saw it all in supreme detail, as if his eye beams were like Madison's telescopes. He watch the burning moonsun, his birthday present from Allah, and Auntie Fatima watch his eyes knowing somehow that she must not disturb him. Uncle Mousse could see the eclipse more clearly, he later say to Auntie, than he could see them in Madison's machines. It was, you see, his eclipse. His eclipse!

"'Mousse,' say Auntie to him. 'Hey! Mousse. You say the white man say it is dangerous to look at this thing. Hey, Mousse. This is too dangerous.' She lead him to the bottom of the knoll. 'Mousse,' say Auntie, 'are you fine?' Uncle Moustapha's eyes were close. He sense that it would be unwise to open them straightaway, though he knew that he could still see. The image of the eclipse was yet in his eyes. It became a lemon, now an emerald, now a circle of evening sky—deep blue, now a violet, a rose and then it fade into darkness. 'Did you see it?' he whisper. 'Did you see my eclipse?'

"'No' say Auntie. 'You tell me on the way here to not look at it. Anyway, it is your gift, you crazy old man. Are you fine? Can you see?'

"'What does it matter? I saw it. My own eclipse.'

"'We must go, old man. You are hungry.'

"So, Marcus, they walk away from the hill. They did not look back. Soon, Moustapha open his eyes and look about him. The whole world was more beautiful to him than ever before. He tell his wife of all that he have seen before, during, and after the eclipse as they walk home. He was happy that he did not obey Madison.

"When they get to the family compound they saw Madison

packing his equipment into his suitcases and Auntie ran to him and speak very fast, but he did not understand. He spoke no Wolof, you see. 'Don't worry about my 'ooman, Mr. Madison,' say Uncle Mousse. 'She is afraid for I look into the eclipse.' Madison almost pull out his hairs when my uncle say this for, as you know, my friend, it was dangerous. 'You crazy man!' say Madison, 'I say not to do this, but you do this. Why?'

"'But I am not blind, Mr. Madison.'

"'One does not have any difficulty seeing after looking directly at an eclipse for a few hours, or even days. You must go see a doctor.' But Uncle Mousse smile only and light a cigarette. He spoke to Madison in the manner of a great imam. 'I will,' he say, 'see today, tomorrow, and always. I have seen what no other living soul have seen today. No, Mr. Madison, no doctor for me.' So Madison finish packing his things, slip some money to Auntie Fatima and went away.

"'What did he say to you?' ask my aunt.

"'He say foolishness,' say Uncle Mousse. 'He tell me to go to the doctor, but I will not. No, I do not care to—.' But he stop short. 'Did you,' he say to Auntie Fatima, 'see a big, black thing fly by to the left of us?'

"'No,' say Auntie.

"'I thought I saw a black shadow fly by us.'

"'Mousse, Mousse, you are going blind. Oyo! Oyo! Ndeysahn. I think I must—.'

"'Fati, stop this. I know what you will say. You old 'ooman, you . . . ' But he was silence again by the dark spot that fly by his vision. It move slower this time and he turn quick to the left to see it, but was gone. 'You saw it again, didn't you, Mousse?' my aunt say with almost crying in her voice.

"'Yes, old 'ooman. Perhap I have make myself blind, indeed. Perhap I should see a doctor.' Auntie insist that Uncle Mousse go to see one of our own marabous because it was the white magic that put him in this situation. Of course, my friend, as you have perhap already guess, Uncle Mousse decide to see a European doctor. He got on the bus to Bassis Santa Su.

"The doctor find Mousse's story incredulous, for he find nothing wrong at all with my uncle's eyes. Nevertheless, Mousse saw the black constantly almost. It flick on and off, on and off in the corner of his left eye. At first it irritate him almost to vexation, but he soon got use to it. The doctor say to him over and over, 'This I don't believe. Your eyesight is excellent except for a slight asti'matism on your left eye.'

"'This I have for years, Doctor Blake. This you already have tell me. Listen, I do not know why I see this little black spot out the corner of my eye; I can still see as before.' He would have say more, but he notice that Dr. Blake was beginning to become too red and his lips look like the lips of a baboon. Very thin and tight. My uncle look at the doctor's eye chart for a moment and then he say, 'Must I return to you?'

"'Yes,' say the doctor. 'I will see you two times more. Come on the tenth and the twentieth, please.'

"'Very good,' say Uncle Moustapha, and he went away.

"Upon arriving to home, Uncle Mousse explain to his wife what the doctor say and ate his lunch with a satisfy smile. Then he retire to his room for his nap. The little black spot follow him to his room like an English lady's dog follow her through town. The room was too warm so he open the window. With the door close and his reading lamp on (my uncle was the first in Sakaam to have electricity and running water in his house), he spread out his mat on the floor and take his Koran to begin his prayer and study before the nap. Everything was silent and still. His heart must have been at peace.

"As he begin to read, he notice that the dark spot no longer flash on and off, but it remain there, hanging in the air. It begin to grow. He was afraid to notice this growing blackness, because he fear it would disappear before he could turn. Or worse yet, would take completely his sight. A sudden chill touch him as the spot grew larger. He spin around violently. His heart pound as he fix his eyes on the giant, black image before him. Without thinking he fumble in his pocket for his cigarettes, offer one to the white hand of his guest, light his own and say to him, 'Been busy lately?'"

"Quite a story," I said to my friend Idi. "And you say it's true?"

"Who knows?" said Idi, lighting a Craven. "You must keep an eye on story-telling Africans."

Gettin to Be Like the Studs

LOUISIANA'S the kind of place that can get cold as hell, or hot as hell, or rain like hell, or windy as hell, but it's usually just hot and sweaty as hell. But that mornin it was cold and it put me in a bad mood. I really don't like this place a whole lot. Besides the crummy weather is the people. The people ain't very friendly and they talk too slow. We got stationed here about six months ago, but I ain't made many friends yet. It ain't like Lackland Air Base over in Texas where we come from. It sure is funny the way you can move somewheres else and people don't even look at you, but in the place you was before, you had lots of friends. This is the kind of place where you got to be real good in some kind of sport, or be real good lookin or like that. Over in Texas, where we was, the thing was for you to have a ghetto blaster and to be able to dance real good and wear nice clothes. I guess I dance pretty good. Not as bad as some guys. I still miss Texas. I wasn't real, real, real popular, but I did OK. To tell you the truth, though, I think I'll be makin more friends now. Now that I got rid of Lenny.

Lenny's a nigger, but for awhile he was my friend. The only friend-friend I've had here so far. Well, he wasn't my best friend or anything. We just usually set on the bus together and made faces and told jokes and junk. Sometimes on weekends we'd throw the ol pigskin around or ride bikes to the base exchange and buy models and stuff like that. We'd build tanks and planes and cars, all kinds. Lenny was pretty good at models. He showed me a lot of neat tricks with paint to make the models real realistic. I thought he was a pretty good guy, and he seemed pretty smart a lot of the time but he was in the slow classes like me. We never had any classes together, though. The only time I ever saw him in school was in the cafeteria, but I never set next to him there. He was the only coon in the whole school.

So anyway, when I walked over to the bus stop that mornin everything was all frosty over. The whole street looked like somebody'd gone berserk with about a hundred cans of fake snow. Everything was white as hell.

I got to the bus stop and there was ol Lenny standin there all by hisself. He really stood out against all that white frost. I guess he was standin there all by hisself cause all the other people out there was girls. He said he didn't like girls, but I knew he did. He was just chicken. He didn't want to get his butt kicked by Buck Tyler or Terry LaPort. Them two guys was the toughest in the whole school and they both hated Lenny's guts. They told him that if they even caught him lookin at any of the girls in school they'd bust his head open. They told him a couple of times, but all Lenny'd ever do was shake his head and say he didn't even like girls. He was such a coward. He wouldn't even admit he liked girls. Sometimes I wanted to bust his head too.

Anyway, I got to the bus stop and just sorta waved to Lenny but I went over and stood next to the girls. I didn't want no one to think I was queer for him or nothin. I like girls, but I'm not a stud like Buck or Terry, I guess. I figure with those guys around the girls didn't have much use for a guy like me. Buck and Terry are the toughest guys you ever seen. Buck's a hellified football player. Boy you shoulda seen how he played against Monroe Jr. Boy, he like to never stop runnin over them punks. He scored three touchdowns and he scored all the extra points. We beat the livin hell outa Monroe and just about everybody else we played. Terry's captain of the football team and also the quarterback. When he threw the ol pigskin the damn thing'd whistle.

Both these guys are always neck-and-neck for top scorer on

the basketball team. And everybody at school says the baseball coach and the track coach, Mr. Deimus and Mr. Meno, are always fightin to get both of em on their teams. See, track and baseball go on at the same time. Girls fight over em too. They got all the chicks they can stand and they get away with just about anything they want at school. They're always pullin some crazy stuff in the cafeteria like puttin salt in somebody's milk or puttin ketchup on somebody's dessert, and stuff like that. Cracks me up. And you think anybody'd do anything about it? Hell no. Once Terry snatched my milk off my tray and drank it down in one gulp. Then he rubbed me on the head and said, "Now what you think a that, pencil neck?" I just looked at him with a mean-looking squint in my eyes, but real fakelike so he could tell I was just playin and wouldn't get mad, and I said, "Do that again, Terry, and I'll just have to buy you another one." Terry pinched me on the cheek and said, "I just bet you would, sweetheart." To be honest, I was a little pissed off by that cause Mom only gives us enough money for one milk a day, but it was pretty funny. At least I didn't say something like, "Duh, that's OK, Terry, I don't even like milk."

So, anyway, I set down on the bus and as usual ol black Lenny sets right down next to me. Boy goddam, I used to hate the way everybody'd hurry to crowd in them seats so they wouldn't have to set with him. And they all treated me like a leper cause I'd aways end up settin next to him. Like it was my job or somethin. That's how I got to know Lenny so good. We'd talk all the way to school and we found out we liked a lot of the same things. After awhile, though, I got pretty tired of settin with the same guy all the time. Especially a colored guy. I tried to set next to ol Big Tim Long once, but he told me he had a real bad cold and that nobody could set next to him. At the next stop, though, Paul Bradford plunked right down next to Tim and Big Tim didn't say one word about havin no cold.

So Lenny sets next to me and right off he starts actin all stupid.

"Hi, Big Ears," he says.

"Oh, hi."

"Man, is it ever cold outside."

"Brilliant one, Sherlock."

"Hey, did you see that new guy sit on the girl's side?"

"Nope."

"Well, he sat next to Cindy Birdsong and she—"

"Everybody makes mistakes. Hey, Lenny, I sorta got this cold. Maybe you should set somewheres else. It's a pretty bad cold."

"A cold ain't gonna kill me, Ears." He was gettin on my nerves. I just couldn't stand to listen to him sometimes. His voice was always quiet like a sissy or somethin and he never cussed or called nobody down. Boy, he was nothin like Buck or Terry. When them guys cussed some fool, he stayed cussed. I remember once Buck called this ol Jewboy down so hard the son of a bitch cried like a baby. Sure, he coulda beat the living crap out of the boy, but when Buck cussed a guy out he didn't need no fisticuffs. This Jewboy, Martin Sharp, was trying to put the moves on Mary Chambeau, this seventh-grader who gots the biggest tits in school. "What's this shit I hear about you trying to droop Mary Chambeau, Sharp?" Buck said to this guy in the locker room. Ol Sharp was standin there with nothin but his towel on him, and you know he wasn't lookin to fight nobody.

Buck's voice can crack like a whip. It's real deep. "What would she want with a Wiener schnitzel like you?" Sharp didn't say nothin. "You no-good, shit-for-breakfast, dog-lookin cock-bite. You so much as look her way again and I'll knock you into next-goddam-week." Sharp's bottom lip started tremblin.

"She talked to me first," ol Jewboy says.

"I don't give a goddam if she proposed to you, Mr. Ziggy Heil. I don't wanna have to tell you twice."

"I don't have to do what you say, Buck."

Then Buck got real tight in Sharp's face, and both of em was all red and puffed up like they was ready to fight. Then Buck says real quiet like a guy in a movie, "If I have to tell you one more time, schnitzel-breath, I'll just rip off your head and yell down your fuckin lungs." And ol Jewboy starts tremblin like mad and tears start rollin down his cheeks. Buck just turns around, grinnin, and struts away. And you think ol Sharp talked to Mary Chambeau after that? But you gotta respect a guy like Sharp for at least standin up some to Buck. Lenny'd never even defend hisself when somebody cussed him. When I asked him why he was so nice to everybody he just gave me that stupid grin of his and says, "Well, you can't fight the whole world." Who's talkin about the whole world?

Well, like I was sayin, there I was, tryin to give him a shove outa my seat and hopefully outa my life, and all he says is, "I don't care if you got a cold. Besides, I don't get sick easy. And anyway, the only other seats are on the girl's side and I ain't sittin over there with them."

"Well why not?"

"You know why."

"Cause you're a faggot."

"You are if I am, elephant ears."

I almost decked him when he called me that. I didn't cause it really didn't bother me all that much if he did it when we wasn't around anyone else. Terry told me once that I shouldn't never let a nigger call me no names. 'Cept it really wasn't just a name. I mean, I really do have pretty big ears. Well, they really ain't all that big. Mom says my ears are prominent. Lenny's got real small ears and I used to call him Little Ears. Big Ears and Little Ears, that's what we'd call each other. A lot of guys at school call me Dumbo. Some girls too. I really don't like that at all, but Terry says they don't mean no harm. But when Lenny called me elephant ears I just got mad as hell and told him to shut up.

We rode along on the bus and everything was real quiet. Nobody said a word. Most people just stared real sleepylike out the windows. Frost was just sprayed all over the place. We passed by the orchard, and everything was all silvery. Even though all the trees in the orchard was fruit trees they all looked like Christmas trees in a way. With bulbs in all. Usually when it wasn't so cold you could smell the fruit and it made your mouth water even if you'd had a big breakfast. I remember when I first got here me and Lenny rode our bikes all the way out to the orchard. Boy, it's a hell of a long way out there by bike. There's a lot of hills out that way and by the time we got there we was beat as all get out.

We had a hell of a good time once we got out there. A hell of a pretty good time, anyway. It was funny, though, the way Lenny and me was hangin on the trees actin like monkeys. Lenny had a pear stuck in his teeth and he was makin monkey noises, hangin upside-down in that tree. I was whoopin and carryin on myself. I did have a peach in my mouth, but it was too green and tasted terrible. I got the idea to play Tarzan and I told Lenny he could be a native or a gorilla and I could fight him, but he said no. He said he didn't wanna be no damn native, cause in Tarzan movies natives always get the crap beat out em. Then he got sorta sad lookin. I felt sorry for him on account of what I said, but then he shouldn't be so damn sensitive.

He was lookin kinda hurt and sensitive when I told him to shut the hell up about my ears, but I was glad he was. I mean, I got tired of that son-of-a-bitch gettin all droopy and sad whenever you said two words about slaves or natives or how it's mainly niggers that brung crack and AIDS into the country and all that. But I guess I'd be embarrassed by all that too if I was colored. I looked at him out of the corner of my eye to see if he was mad at me. "Lenny," I says to him, "How's it feel bein the only colored guy in school?"

"I'm used to it," he said. "I don't really mind. It was like this when we were stationed in Nebraska. Besides . . . nobody really bothers me."

"Oh yeah? Well as for myself, I couldn't stand it."

"How come?"

"Cause I'd just want to be around my own kind." I was tryin

to let him down easy. But he was too dumb to get my message. He just set there lookin out the window.

"Well," he said back, "what's so great about bein around your own kind?"

"I don't know. Cause you'd be a lot better off. Look, you're the only colored guy in the whole school. You can't have no girlfriends. The fellas wouldn't let you on none of the sports teams. Nobody sits by you at lunch. Hell, you don't even have a locker partner. Everybody calls you names, Lenny, and you let em. I myself couldn't stand it. I just couldn't stand it. If I was you I'd ask my folks to let me transfer to Washington over in downtown. I myself couldn't stand it, not being around my own kind."

He didn't say nothin for the longest time. He just set there and nodded his big black head. Then he looked up and stared me right in the eyes. He started talkin and his voice was real, real quiet. Quieter than I ever heard it. "So tell me something, Ears," he said. "How much goddam better off are you, man?" He said some more stuff, but I wasn't listenin. Couldn't stand that mousey voice of his no more.

The bus pulled up to the school and we got off. Everybody got off real zombielike. I hopped off the steps and walked away from Lenny as fast as I could. I tried to lose him in the crowd. I didn't run cause you can get in trouble for runnin on school grounds. But I was movin like a blue blaze and I figured I'd lost him. I stood in line and hoped I'd got my point across to him. But when I turned around, there he was standin right there behind me. I turned away real fast so no one could tell we was together. When I turned, though, I seen Buck's big, blond head way up to the front of the line. I thought he seen me too. I didn't want him to see me there next to Lenny. Lenny was standin there looking all dumb and niggery, and then he tapped me on the arm and said, "Well, only two more days of school and then it's Saturday, Ears." I didn't say nothin at first and then I turned around real fast and boy I let him have it.

"Why don't you quit followin me, dog."

He just looked at me and grinned. I guess he thought I was playin.

"Get the hell away from me," I said. "You always follow me around like a damn dog. Is that what you are, a damn, stupid dog? Ya dog." I had to say it loud enough so Buck could hear me. "Get away from me, dog. Ya act like a damn dog followin me around. Ya make me sick as hell."

I thought he was gonna hit me at first cause his eyes got real tight lookin, and for a second there I got a little scared. He had his fist all balled up and he looked like he wanted to kill me. Then he looked around him and all the people in line who heard me was howlin and barkin like dogs and laughin like a son of a bitch. Then Lenny's eyes got all sad and worried-lookin and I thought for sure he was gonna cry. But he just stood there, shakin like a leaf.

The bell rung and the line started movin for the door. I walked on but Lenny just stood there lookin stupid. I have to admit he did look pretty pitiful, like Jewboy Sharp. A few people were still makin dog noises at him, but he didn't do nothin. He just stood there, lookin down at his big feet. I guess everybody thought it was pretty funny. It was, in a way. When I got to the front door I turned around to see if I could see ol Lenny but he wasn't around nowhere. Then Buck come runnin up to me and slapped me on the shoulder. He was crackin up. "Damn, Dumbo," he said to me, "you sure did put that jig in his place, didn't you?"

"Yeah, I guess I did."

"You sure as hell did, Dumbo. I was pretty worried about you for awhile there, boy." He slapped me on the shoulder again and walked off into the buildin, lookin tough as all get out. I looked back to see ol Lenny, but he wasn't around. I tried like hell to be nice to him. I tried to shake him loose and not be too obvious about it. But Terry LaPort says you can't be too nice to them people. He said they got brains as small as golf balls inside skulls as hard as brick. I guess he's right.

Anyway, I felt pretty good about the whole thing. Cause even though I called him down and got him away from me for good, I think I was pretty decent about it. I mean, I didn't hit him or call him nigger which woulda really been hard on him.

He really would be better off with his own kind. Everybody is. Like me. I really ain't made no real friends yet, no friend-friends. But Buck and them says yo to me every now and then. They're pretty friendly when you get on their good side. I know them and me'll get real tight one day. Cause since I cussed out ol black Lenny, I'm gettin to be a hell of a lot more like the studs every day.

"I am, I am obsessed
With all these little things
It's such a crying shame"

The Voice

MY father once told me that if I should ever steal I should never steal from the rich. "Only steal from poor folks," he said. His reasoning was that the rich are intimately aware of every single thing they own. "Michael, you take so much as a needle and thread from a rich fella," he said, "and he and his hounds'll be at your door so fast it'll make your head spin." But stealing from the poor is different. The poor are only aware of what they lack, and all they own is fair game for even the clumsiest thief. Of course, my father was really asking me not to steal at all. Stealing from the rich would lead you into misery, while stealing from the poor makes you feel miserable.

To this day, I don't know why I took The Voice's song. It seemed to be just about the only thing he had. When I took his song away from him I might have even taken away his dreams. But it was my intention, at the very first, to invite him in some night and have him record his song for me. I used to think, "Wouldn't it be nice if the whole world could hear his song rather than just a lucky few down on Pendleton Avenue?" I wanted him to sit down with me, have a couple of beers and do that beautiful, unworldly song of his. God! What a song.

It was really ten songs. Or, at least, it seemed like ten songs at first. But I found out later that you couldn't cut it up into a bunch of little three-minute tunes which could be spoon-fed to the masses over the Top 40 airwaves. That's what I had in mind in the beginning, but I found out later that cutting up that song would be like cutting up Handel's *Water Music* or the *Brandenburg Concerti.* Those "songs" The Voice did weren't songs at all. It was an opera, or a symphony, I guess you could say, intricately pieced together, movement by movement. If you put the second movement before the first, the fifth where the seventh should be, and so on, you'd end up with some flat, unappealing hodgemess of pretty colors and meaningless vibrations.

Then too, it was the way he sang it. The range of his voice was astounding. It was hard to say how many octaves he had balled up in his tiny, burned-out, brown body. But give him a note and I'd bet you twenty dollars on a ten dollar bill he could hit it. He sang so effortlessly. He sang the same way he walked, part gliding, part rolling, part shuffling down from Polk Street all the way to Weir Point, nodding to keep time in that lazy, liquid way of his.

What can I say? He was the greatest singer I've ever heard. Maybe, if there is such an animal, the greatest singer alive. I don't know. Any metaphor I could use to describe his voice—honey, lightning, wind, fire, drum, string, flute—would be pitiful understatement. When he sang you'd lie there in bed as if pinned down with this lambent feeling in your stomach. You felt as if he'd opened your stomach and filled it with a soft orange-red light that carried every sensation and every emotion that people are capable of feeling.

I'm such a little thang
It's such a cryin shame
I am I am obsessed . . .

I couldn't get The Voice to come up and record so much as a fart. You'd call out to him from the window and all he'd ever do was smile and wave, never missing a note. People would throw coins at his feet and he'd maybe stop and turn to whatever direction the money had come from and sing a few bars, but never stoop to pick up the money. He was obviously poor, but he never took a dime.

He didn't come every night or even with any kind of regularity. It might sound weird, but he seemed to come when you needed him. When you needed him he was right there, singing infinity into your stomach. I don't really know exactly what I mean by "he came when you needed him." He just came at all the right times. On the nights he came you could feel his presence before you actually heard him. The air carried all the stillness of those moments just before the bellowing of a hurricane or the howling of a tornado. The air would be stiff, quivering. I swear, babies wouldn't cry, phones wouldn't ring, you wouldn't hear stereos, appliances, barking mutts, TVs. It was so quiet you could almost hear him inhaling before he blew that first note.

So I knew he was coming, that night. I had my mikes and recorders ready. I stood on the corner of Polk and Pendleton, listening to the empty street. A couple of times I switched on a recorder prematurely. You see, once you'd heard the guy sing, sometimes you hear him even when he's not there. It's not like some pop tune idly circling through your head, but almost like he's there. Only more hollow-sounding, perhaps. It was the only song that mattered to you once you'd heard it. The only one you ever hummed to yourself when you felt like humming. I'd always know when I was around a neighbor when walking through a mall or some such place. I'd hear a snatch of that song coming from somewhere, turn and smile at the person and he or she'd smile back, wink, or nod, give me the thumb or whatever.

It was cold that night and I was a little worried my equipment would give me problems. Like an idiot, I was standing there saying, "Testing—testing, are you there?" into my mikes when I heard the first notes of his song.

ooh ooh, la la la la
I got the singin seed
I got the singin seed . . .

I was so rattled I threw my recorder into fast-forward, like a dummy, panicked and fumbled thirty precious seconds away.

. . . can you tell me
If I'm comin from
Or if I'm goin to . . .

I got things straight and ran as silently as I could, which wasn't so silent with all the junk I was carrying, to close the gap that had spread between us. Of course that screwed things up even more, but soon I was within decent range. He never heard me.

I'm such a little thang
Lord, it's a cryin shame
I am I am obsessed

obession without tears
obession without fears
ooh ooh la la la la . . .

For all the screw-ups I'd made early on, the tape came out beautifully. My equipment wasn't too sophisticated, mind you, but it was good. The whole process of making the tape presentable took months. I discovered that ordinary noise reduction was an inadequate method for eliminating background noises so I had to shell out several hundred dollars to get the tape computer-cleaned, a method that a musician friend developed a half dozen years or so ago. Then I had to hire a good band to add some background vocals, a little violin here, cello there, percussion, guitar. But not too much. I wanted it to sound sort of spare. I wanted to keep that orange-red sound of infinity.

I tried for weeks, without success, to push the song. I sent tapes to WABC out East, KJOQ out West, WOW in the Midwest. I sent tapes to any recording artist I figured could do justice to the song: Betty Carter, Bobby McFerrin, James Taylor, Ricky Lee Jones, Ella Fitzgerald. I sent copies everywhere, knowing what a risk I was taking. I was sure that The Voice had never even thought of giving the song a copyright and I didn't want to get caught trying to pull a fast one. But I figured what the hell; it's for a good cause. I had the thing copyrighted under a pseudonym: Buster Williby. I sent out, I guess, around thirty copies of the tape to the four corners. There were no takers, no buyers, no phone calls, no letters, no nothing, nowhere. It's as if I'd sent blank tapes to the deaf.

The band, this group called The Leg, who'd helped me with the accompaniment, kept bugging me to sell them the song. But I wasn't about to turn it over to a second-rate rock band who couldn't guarantee me they'd be able to take the song, as well as the rest of their big-yawn repertoire, any farther than Coco's Night Bird over on West and Gilford. They were decent enough musicians, but I wanted the song to go straight to the top with as few risks as possible. But they kept on pushing me, telling me that the song wouldn't have been presentable if they hadn't had a hand in things. That's when I decided to cut the song into little pieces.

Take the clouds out from the sky
and you'll see clearer things
you won't see nearer things

Take your mind off what you do
Then you will understand
It wasn't mind, but hand . . .

"You think they liked it?"

"Sure, Mike. Sure they liked it."

"Yeah, yeah, but I mean, they didn't seem gassed. It didn't hit em like it should have."

"Well, what did you expect?"

"Skip it."

"What's the matter with you?"

"Never mind. Just skip it."

"Goddam, man, you act like it's your tune."

"Don't call it a tune, it's not a tune."

"Oh Jesus Hotel. Here, have some of this."

"Get that crap out of my face. You guys ruined it. You can't hold a candle to him."

"Him who?"

"You know goddam well who."

"Hey, quit jabbin me with your finger. You ain't no gym coach. Lighten up, Mike. Jesus Hotel, man, it's our tune now. We'll do it however we want. If you want it sung the way the guy sings it, go get him. We did it alright. They danced, didn't they? Don't be so tense."

"They weren't supposed to dance. They were supposed to listen. For once. Just once they were supposed to listen. That song is supposed to do something to you. You dorks can't do it right then don't do it at all. You don't have any idea at all, do you? You ain't got one idea. You can't hear and you don't care—"

"Hey—"

"I knew I shouldn't have let you guys do it. You and all these flashing lights, and all this third-rate sound equipment can't even, don't even begin to hold a candle to some little skin and bones nigger who can't even afford a mega-goddamn-phone. You go up on that stage and try to rock these lowlife geeks who can't even see straight enough to slam dance, for Christ's sake. Forget about it. Just forget about it."

It's such a little thang
It's such a cryin shame . . .

Weeks and weeks and weeks went by and The Voice hadn't come down Pendleton at all. It was midsummer, a time, it seemed, when everybody needed him most. People would sit on their stoops obviously waiting for him, but never admitting so. I started to feel like a criminal. I was, in a way. I began to carry around this ugly, knotted-up feeling whenever somebody would so much as glance my way.

The Voice

It's such a cryin shame . . .

"Where do you think he is, Mike?"

"How should I know? He came here like from nowhere. Maybe he's gone back to nowhere."

"More coffee? Sure would be nice if he came around soon. The place seems so hollow at night."

"Yeah, thanks. Well, hell, maybe he signed a recording contract out on the West Coast."

"No, not him."

"Why not him? We don't know. Nobody around here knows the guy."

"He just isn't the kind of man to go running off to California to become a recording star. You've seen what he does when people try to give him money."

"Chump change. I'd do the same thing, Betty. But walk up to him with a fat check and a contract and he'd change his tune."

"A song like that and a voice like that were never meant to be on vinyl. My mother thinks he's an angel of God."

"Oh, for crying out loud, Betty—"

"I didn't say I believe her, or agree with her . . . but you have to admit he's not like anything anyone's ever heard. I wouldn't be surprised if any recording you tried to make of him came out blank."

"Yeah, me neither. Hey, speaking of music, did you catch that Bruce Hornsby concert on channel 86 last Tuesday?"

"No, I didn't. Sure hope he comes back. Sure would be nice."

"Yeah. Well, I've gotta scoot, Betty. Thanks for the coffee and everything."

I turned my shoulder to the sun
It over-shadowed everyone
The angry soldier raised the gun
And shot the hero-pilot . . .

He did come out of nowhere on a Friday night in late October three years ago. The moon cut into the sky like a big crystal thumbnail behind a gauzy, glowing cloud. It looked like a scene from a werewolf movie. The air was tense and still as it always would be just before he came strolling. You could tell something was going to happen.

When I heard his opening notes I was at my IBM trying to design plans for a new computer game based on the movie "Midnight Express," a game that would have all the usual death, destruction, beating of breast, and gnashing of teeth. I was bored to two or three shades of gray, trying to decide whether the Billy Hayes subprogram should be given two escape routes from the isolation pit or just one. Then, somewhere in the middle of my fifth debugging session, The Voice touched me. The odd thing was that the words didn't seem to come from outside, bounce around my inner ear and all that. They seemed to come from inside me as if they were my own thoughts. The warm orange-red flowed from the center of my brain to the middle of my stomach. My legs turned to liquid. I felt an impulse to say something or do something, but the impulse was so mixed around that I felt like I had to do everything, whatever it was, all at once. All I could do was sit there and let the music do whatever it was doing to me. After several long moments I felt myself slide from my desk and move to the window. I saw the little black man gliding down the middle of the street, vapor steaming out his mouth, head rolling and nodding on a scrawny neck like an ancient Stevie Wonder made of ashes and black silk. The song was much bigger than he. It seemed to come from beneath him, from deep, deep under the ground and push into every corner of space.

I hope ya'll understan
I hope ya'll understan
ooh ooh la la la la

Still trying to push the song, I went to all but two radio stations in town. Nobody gave me even two seconds of time. My nerves were shot and I started screwing up something awful at work. No new ideas would come to me. All I could think about was The Voice. I saw my friends less and less often. I did every drug I could get my hands on.

I am I am obsessed . . .

"Well, what's wrong with you?"

"Nothing, Kirsten. Skip it."

"Skip hell. Who is she?"

"What?"

"Look, Mike, I ain't no kid. If you're screwin somebody else just tell me and quit wastin my time."

"Who says . . . What do you mean, what's wrong with me? What's wrong with you? Who says I'm screwing around on you?"

"Oh, get real. Your mouth, your hands, your eyes, everything. You think you're talkin to some kid? Just cause I'm nineteen don't mean I don't know what's goin on. You're always broke. You never call me. I ain't stupid.

"For Christ—Look, Kirsten, I've just been working too hard. I'm tired. I do have a right to be tired, don't I?"

"Not for no six months, Mike. That's real original, Mike. Tired."

"Why don't you go stuff yourself, bimbo."

"Good suggestion, ass-wipe. Don't call. Don't write, and don't come by, I'm walkin."

There I was in Africa
Without a taste of shade
Without my cutting blade

Like I said there were only two radio stations left in town for me to try. I wasn't happy about either one, but I didn't have much choice either. There was KCMO, a classical station that I suspected wouldn't play the song under threat of terrorism. That left KCRR, the local college station. They'd play damned near anything, but had only a handful of listeners. Their format was never the same from month to month as they were an experimental station always trying to out-avant every garde that ever crawled out of the gutter. But what could I do? I called the station manager and begged her to give me an appointment. "I'm kind of busy with midterms," she said. "You can send me your tape, but I won't be able to get back to you for awhile."

Midterms.

Some four months before I'd been reduced to the likes of KCRR, The Leg had, it appeared, struck it fairly big on the national music market. Three of their songs had made it to the bottom of the Top 100 charts. One of them was a cover of "Johnny Angel," all waved-up and full of synthesizers. The other two were ghastly covers of parts of The Voice's song. One was the movement I let them "have" way back when. The other was a movement they'd apparently scratched up from their feeble, coked-out memories. The songs had gone through so much electronic mutation that they were barely recognizable. It still pissed me off that they'd stolen what I was absolutely convinced, by then, was mine. But there was so little resemblance between "my" song and theirs that I still thought I had every reason in the world to be relatively optimistic.

Obsession without fears . . .

"Look, my friend, I don't know how you got past my secretary, but I'm not gonna—"

"For Christ's sake, just listen to it. Listen to the goddamn thing."

"Now look. I'm gonna tell you just one more time, red, and then I'm gonna ask you to leave. Radio in the eighties just don't work like this anymore. Every millisecond of air time is spoken for. You just don't stroll into a radio station like KMIK, and throw down some cheapo cassette—"

"Who says it's cheap? Hey, man, all I'm asking—"

". . . down on the program director's desk and say, 'Oh, jeepers, this is the greatest little number that ever . . . '"

"Can I leave it?"

"' . . . a body sung'—Hell no, you can't leave it here. Do you have any idea what goes into some sound—any sound—on the air? Pally, you have no idea. Obviously, you have no idea. You got . . . "

"Skip it."

". . . about a million sponsors competing, paying top dollar to target . . . "

"Skip it! Skip it! Just forget about it."

". . . the right kind of ad for the right kind of . . . "

I was fired from my job for many reasons, but I think what vexed management most was that I spent all my time at work programming just about every computer on my floor to play the song. They tell me it took thousands of dollars to unscrew the computers. At first I was given what they called administrative leave to pull myself into one piece, but I told the board members to go suck something or other. Right away I moved into a little roach farm off Weir. Every night I'd walk up to Pendleton, stand on the corner and wait for The Voice. But he never came.

Then he did come. In a way.

He came just when I'd figured he was dead, or had left town. I was broke, hungry, and a little more than bitter. All the sacrifices I'd made. All the work. After losing my job, my girlfriend, my apartment, I figured enough was enough. I wanted to make some money. I figured I had it coming to me. Well, hell, I did. I really did. I mean, what would you do if you were, say, out walking in the woods or something and you came upon an old, ignorant farmer who owned a few acres that were crammed full of gold? And each time you observed him out there you saw him breaking his back on all those huge golden chunks.

And what would you think if you saw him spit and curse while grabbing those chunks and heaving them out of the plow's path so he could break his back for some pitiful-ass barley or rutabagas or some such trash?

You'd take all the gold to Washington so the president could balance the budget. Or give it to the poor, buy the farmer a tractor, build libraries and dams. Yeah, I'm sure.

So there I was, one night, pacing the thirty-year-old carpet in my little apartment, rubbing my mitts together like a housefly on swill. I would sue the living pants off The Leg for stealing, then wrecking my song. After winning in court, and after all the predictable media attention, my God, I'd release the song. The coin would roll. But I wouldn't be greedy, I thought. Being wealthy and all, I'd hire a private eye or two and find The Voice. And when he was found, I'd give him, say, a quarter of what I'd earned, maybe buy him a home, put him up for the rest of his life. It would be good for him. It would be nice.

But the old boy found me.

I was pacing, and felt the quiet, the air stiffen, dogs and TVs clam up. The usual. I stepped to the window, leaned out, waited. Sheer anticipation set my teeth on edge, made my stomach tickle, my ears tremble. Silence pressed my skull like great black hands. I waited; the earth waited.

Nothing.

Nothing.

Nothing.

And it stayed so all night long. Nothing could have been more painful. Not interrupted coitus, not unrequited love, not the vacuum of death. Nothing. I tossed in bed all night long, till the sunlight bled in through my filthy venetian blinds. I slipped from bed, moved to the window and peered out. I saw the old man, The Voice, standing on the sidewalk below. Will he sing? I asked myself. He wore a black fedora and an old raincoat. His hands were in his pockets, the hat tipped back. We stared at each other, our eyes locked together, our bodies as motionless as those small animals you see frozen in the glare of oncoming headlights. Will he sing? I felt the orange-red stoke up in my viscera. I imagined new lyrics, sadder music, cursing me, my theft, those like me who would ham-handedly bury black artists while beatifying their art. Finally, he inhaled deep and slow, his shoulders lifting with the effort. Will he sing? He held that breath for an eternity; I held my breath too, my veins drubbing my temples. And then, almost imperceptibly, he lowered his chin toward his chest, and sighed an ice-cold northeaster of a sigh. I felt its silent force against chest, it rattled through my bones, numbed my fingertips. The Voice shook his head, then turned away and stepped down Weir. And all the goddam while I kept asking, Will he sing? Will he ever sing?

I set my heels and rolled my eyes
Up to the pale, unblinking skies
I tried to catch ya'll's culture train
But memories took me back again

"Hello? Mike Baer?"

"Yeah?"

"Mary Brink from KCRR here."

"Yeah? Yeah, hi."

"Man you sure are hard to get a hold of. Hey listen, I'm just calling to tell you what a success your song has been on our station."

"Yeah?"

"Oh definitely. People keep calling, asking us to play it over and over. It's totally phenomenal. Everybody here is, like, freaked. It's really a stiff tune. Just thought I'd call you to let you know. And, um, are you on a label yet? We'd really like to have some more of your stuff. It's really phenomenal."

"Well . . . thanks, but it's just sort of a hobby with me. I honestly never thought about a label."

"Well you should. Oh, listen. I just had a talk with Dave

Clemmons, the head of the Folk/Jazz/Rock Committee here at the college and he's, like, been wanting to ask you to do a concert at Bond Hall here on campus sometime this winter. He'd have sent you a letter, but you didn't leave an address, and, like I said, you're really hard to reach by phone."

"Well, my phone had been disconnected up until about last Tuesday. I've had a pretty tough time with money, lately. But, anyway, as for the concert . . . well . . . it may not sound like it but I have this real bad cold. Lost my singing voice. Don't think I'll be singing for awhile. I'll get back with you."

Obsession without tears
Obsession without fears . . .

Pretty soon things got completely out of my hands. What good would it have done me to continue claiming the song was mine? I can't even carry a tune. I don't know the first thing about music. I slunk into a silent anonymity as quickly as my feets could carry me. The world owned the song after all. The song became so popular on KCRR that people began wondering why they weren't hearing it on other stations. The other stations, quite naturally, couldn't dig it up at first, but I guess, by either pirating straight off the college station or making some kind of deal with Mary Brink, or one of her employees, they got it. Every one of them got it. You heard it on the radio morning, noon, and night. It's all you'd ever hear. They'd announce the song as "Cryin' Shame" by a mysterious group called Obsession.

In no time the song was number one statewide, and it floated from state to state. It was a national hit inside a year. There was great speculation as to whom this group, Obsession, actually was. Some people said that the John Lennon murder had, in fact, been a hoax, and that in truth, he'd gone underground for several years to work on his greatest song ever. Similar theories were purported with credit to Jimi Hendrix, Jim Morrison, Sid Vicious, for Christ's sake, and a host of other deceased rock stars. Some people said it was a collaboration, heretofore unknown, between Gershwin and Ellington which had been lost in the National Jazz Archives and rescued by one David "Sweet Pea" Hollins of Warner Brothers records. (Warner Brothers somehow usurped the rights to the song, and were evidently enjoying the myths concocted as much as the money made. They made six million dollars alone from elevator music companies.) My favorite myth was the one about the song being the work of an eight-year-old blind and deaf idiot savant from the Appalachian hills named Buster Williby.

Well, some said this and some said that and the song stayed number one on the Billboard charts for thirty-nine consecutive weeks, an all-time record. It fell to number three and hovered there for eight weeks, then fell to number thirty-seven, staying there for nearly a month. It went off the charts in February of last year. I don't recall ever having heard it again.

The Honey Boys

HE jabbed me with that goddamned pointy-ass elbow. He did it all the time. Every two seconds whether he had your attention or not. He'd jab your ribs or needle your arm till you'd flail as if fighting off mosquitoes in a dark room. "Hey, Spider—hey, man," he said. "You heard the one about the colored guy who goes—"

"Black. How many times I gotta tell you? Black."

"Well, I can't get used to it. When I was in elementary we used to call you guys black to cut you down."

"You'll get over it. Go ahead with the joke."

"OK," he said. "So this black guy goes into a barber shop, and the barber says to him, 'What can I do for you, sir?' And the guy says, 'I want that afro look. Gimme the afro look,' you know? So while the black guy's sitting in the barber chair he falls asleep, and when he wakes up, you know? He's got this big honkin' bone through his nose."

The boy went berserk. His mouth opened suitcase wide. His teeth shone like yellow piano keys. He had big bucked teeth, and when his lips sheeted them he looked like a Camel. So I called him Camel. But not to his face. "Get it?" he said, damned near choking himself. "A bone through his nose." He kept jabbing while he cackled. I hoped he'd work himself into a seizure.

"Old one," I said, and walked away.

I hated playing straight man to him but I always did. I didn't like him, yet I say he was my best friend. I was just that way. I was an Army brat and I'd been to fifteen different schools by the time I was sixteen. As a result I seldom connected with people. I could adapt like a chameleon, but never cohere. But I told lies that most high-school-aged boys don't tell. Most of them blather about girls they've "nailed" or "poked" or "drilled" or "popped" or "drooped." They tally up their countless touchdowns, their innumerable knockout punches, their uncountable miles-per-hour, their interminable trips to the keg. But I told people that my birthday was in September, while in truth, it is in May. I told people I was a pessimist, when really I was the most optimistic person I knew. I am a Jew, yet few of my "closest friends" knew a thing about my conversion. Instead, most of them thought I had Buddhist leanings. I would tell them I wore a size eleven-and-a-half shoe, when in truth my shoe size was twelve. I told people I was born in Tennessee. That was a lie. I told them my mother smoked filterless cigarettes. That was a lie. I told them I was allergic to raisins. I loved raisins. I told people I had dysgraphia. I had dyslexia. I drew myself in fuzzy lines, always smudging, but rarely highlighting. But things were a little different for me with Camel. For some reason I could unflinchingly tell him the truth about myself, everything, from the moment I met him. But I never told him I didn't like him. That's one thing I never did.

I met the Camel my first day at Palmer High in Colorado Springs. It was a nice day. Lots of sun. Lots of girls in shorts. I don't know why I decided to go out for football. If I hadn't it's hard to say whether I would have ever met the Camel. I'd promised myself I wouldn't make the same mistakes at this school I'd made at the others. I was going to make good grades this time. I'd always had a rotten time with academics. I'd gotten into the habit of meeting people through athletics. I didn't say making friends, I said meeting people. Everybody needs someone to tell him which teachers to avoid, where to find summer work, where to find good pot, if that's your sort of thing. (It was certainly mine.) I needed allies. And I knew no better conduit to alliance than sports. Consequently, I spent so much time trying to make a decent athlete of myself that my grades fell by the wayside, as my father put it.

I signed up for football anyway. Reflex, I guess. And my parents, for some reason or another, never objected. When that first practice ended I felt like quitting. I was in terrible shape. I sat in front of my locker, too tired to respond to the pointy elbow that prodded my arm.

"Hey, soul brother. Some practice, eh? You new? What position ya play? Play defensive end, myself. I played last year, but I didn't letter. I played the year before too, but that was freshman ball. I started. Didn't even play in eighth grade. Man's gotta play to get the chicks, right, soul brother? We oughta have a baaad team this year, my man. Lots of soul brothers on the team. Hey, how come you guys are so good in sports? Are you my size? Stand up so I can see . . . ." He went on like this while I sat there and wheezed. After awhile I looked up at this big, tall bird with his long face and big teeth. He seemed nice, but I couldn't see him making a valuable ally. He looked too straight. I let him go on till he shut up, then excused myself. I was the last one in the shower and the last one out.

I expected the locker room to be empty when I left the shower room. But when I got back, there he stood in high-water corduroys and a plaid shirt, his hair whipped into a wet pompadour. "What took you so long, soul brother?" he said. "Thought you drowned."

"Look, call me Spider."

"Spider?"

It's my nickname. My real name's Stuart, but it sounds too formal and I hate to be called Stu."

"Spider's OK. My name's Caspar."

We shook.

"Caspar?" I said. "Jesus Christ."

"Hey, man, don't take the Lord's name in vain."

"His name's Caspar?"

"I'm not kidding."

"Well, you said . . . "

"I'm serious, man." He looked at the floor as he said this and I was a little worried that I'd really offended him. Then suddenly, he looked up with a smile. "Ya got a couple a minutes to go somewhere with me?" he said. I told him I had to catch the activity bus. "You can take the late one," he said. "Just want you to meet a couple a my good friends."

"No, I don't think so."

"Come on, soul . . . Spider, man. You'll really like these people. They're really mellow. Freaked out on Jesus. Bunch a good dudes, man. Like Jerry. Jerry's cool. He used to do junk, but the Lord freaks him out more'n drugs now, man. Come on, Spy."

He called me Spy.

"Come on, man," he said. "It won't take long." He stood very close to me. His saliva pelted me as he rattled on about his friends. The usual Godspiel. People messed up on drugs in the sixties, messed up on the Lord in the seventies. I tried to be discreet about wiping his cloudburst off my face. I don't know why I try so damned hard not to embarrass people by pretending not to notice what slobs they are. I'm the famous I-always-apologize-when-people-step-on-my-feet type you always read about in advice columns. The little gray people who sometimes wind up shooting presidents or holding Bell Telephone employees hostage for some ineffable reason. But they usually do nothing. The world is full of Mittys who do nothing. They dream, of course, of leaping on hand grenades on crowded streets and saving five hundred lives. They dream of all sorts of exuberant, nut-busting aggressiveness but would sooner commit *sepuku* than tell mindless slobs like Caspar to quit spitting all over the damned place and no I won't go with you and meet your pathetic, burned-out friends.

So.

On the way to meet his friends he asked me if I knew the Lord.

"If you mean J.C., no," I said. "I'm Jewish."

He stopped walking, grabbed my arm. "Wow, a black Jew," he said. "It must be tough with two strikes against you like that." I didn't reply. What could I have said to him? I thought of saying, Wow, a white Christian. It must be a real thrill to have everything in your favor. But that would have hurt his feelings. Still, his remark bothered me. He was standing there holding my arm, looking at me as if I'd told him I'd been born without sex organs. I thought, here I am with this obnoxious dimwit and he's got *me* down two strikes. Jesus Christ on a stick. Of course, I could have lied in the usual way. I could have said, Yes, Caspar, it hurt, man. It hurt real, real deep, and I be grievin sometimes. But it never crossed my mind.

"It must be real tough," he said again.

"Where is this place we're supposed to be going to?"

"Do you believe in God, Spy?"

"Oh please, man. Do you want me to go with you to this place, or not?"

"I just axed a question. I don't know much about your religion except you don't eat ham, pork chops, baloney, and stuff like that."

"Well, I'll give you a book on it or something. Where is this place we're going?" We resumed our walk, but at a much slower pace. He didn't say anything for at least two blocks and then he nudged me with the elbow, and said, "You know Sammy Davis, Jr.'s Jewish and he seems pretty happy."

What could I have said to him? I turned my attention from the Camel and spied the city. Colorado Springs was never my favorite city. It's kind of a town-city, really. That's part of what I never liked about it. It can't make up its mind what it wants to be. It's big. Or I should say spread out. Wider than Brazil, but there aren't any buildings. Not any big ones, anyway. I hated it. I liked a place with tall buildings. Colorado Springs, as big as it is, is full of these timid, squatty, cowering things of red brick or brownstone. It's like this herculean body with the head of a shrew. And the streets are as wide as the Oklahoma panhandle, as if they were built for cars that run sideways. There's nothing intimate about the place. Makes you feel exposed.

And the people.

Christ, the people.

They can't make up their minds either. They want to be townlike, but they usually end up citylike. You walk into a Safeway and people try to chat with you about the weather or boy-them-Broncos. They smile and give you all this you-have-a-nice-day-and-come-back-and-see-us and blah, blah, blah, but they do it as if every nerve in their bodies rebelled against it. They stand behind their counters stiff as sign posts with these pathetic terror-grins on their faces, heads cocked, eyes doing all kinds of intricate acrobatics so as not to come into contact with so much as your shirt collar.

The Camel wasn't like that at all. He was all town. A Turkish town maybe. Always in your face, crowding you in all that immense space. Grabbing. Nudging. Jabbing. As we walked down the boulevardlike sidewalk he kept bumping into me. I tried to put some space between us by moving to my left, but he stuck to me like a defensive back. He put his hand on my shoulder and asked me, "Hey, you're not mad at me, are you, soul brother?"

"Why would I be mad at you?"

"You tell me. Everybody gets pissed at me for some reason or another. I say hi to people and they get all bent out a shape. It happens all the time. I remember when I was in third grade this sixth grader, a big black guy—no offense—snatched my sandwich from me and squished it in his hand. For no reason. I wasn't even sitting at his table. Never saw the guy before. He just came out a nowhere and wrecked my sandwich. Stuff like that always happens to me . . . . People I meet for the first time call me goofy or dufus or something. What is it, my breath or something?" He had bad breath. "I'm a friendly guy."

"Seem like it to me. Is this place much farther?"

"Just a couple a blocks. You think I'm friendly?"

"Oh yeah."

"Well, why do people always mess with me?"

"Maybe they're just jealous."

"People treat you like that cause you're a black Jew?"

"Depends. My parents rag on me, sometimes."

My family isn't Jewish, of course, just me. I was a Jew, anyway. I stopped practicing Judaism several years ago. It got too hard. It was too lonely. Black people would accuse me of trying to run away from my history. Jewish people would keep a quiet, embarrassed-for-you distance from me, particularly the secular Jews. Perhaps they felt uncomfortable because I'd embraced something that had often brought them a great deal of pain. I could practice Judaism and still never really be a Jew.

I converted when I was sixteen. I am, to this day, a Jew on paper, but after ten years of looking inside and outside myself, I decided I wasn't so hot at "Jewing." Maybe I converted for all the wrong reasons. Who knows?

Before my father's Fort Carson assignment we lived in Montgomery, Alabama. I was the only black kid attending Green Acres Junior High. It was the first time in my life I'd ever been spat on, beat up for talking to white girls, cut from every athletic team I tried out for. It was a long time before I even realized why I was anathema to those kids, coaches, and teachers, and even longer before I found an ally. David Vegod. They picked on Dave too, but not (at first, anyway) because he was a Jew. Dave looked Asian. Dave was an air force brat. Dave was an oddball. They called him the Flying Yang From Outerspace. He busted neck veins denying his Asianness, asserting his Jewishness, and naturally, they ate him up. They called him every name in the box, and when he and I became friends they called him nigger lover.

It's simple enough. I converted because Dave was a nigger lover. Because neither he nor his God were rednecks. His God wanted you to study, learn, grow up, affirm life, defend friends.

You could talk to this guy's God, argue with him, even, without the supplications of some cosmic mouthpiece. I had grown to despise all those tract-toting schmucks who were so concerned about my not having a "personal r'lationship with th' Lard," while not a damned one of them ever stopped to consider having a personal relationship with me. But little of their hypocrisy mattered to me after my conversion. I was Dave's buddy, God's chosen, stronger inside and out. I was no longer simply the "onliest coon in the whole school." I was unique. But it's really hard to be more specific about the reasons for my conversion. It's like explaining why you've fallen in love with someone. You can't really explain. All you can really say is that she brings out something in you that nobody else does.

As Caspar and I walked, I wanted to tell him what it was like to be me, that though being both black and Jewish could be difficult, it brought out something in me nothing else did. Sometimes it *was* hard. My parents, depending on their mood, would laugh about my conversion, pretend it never happened, or taunt me at the dinner table with, "Can you people eat this? Can you people eat that?"And it stung me when people would say things like, "What? You don't look Jewish. Did you get a nose job too?" And I'd grown so tired of people bringing up Sammy Davis, Jr., when they learned of my faith, as if his existence legitimized my very being, made the unlikely likely. Brother Sammy tainted my uniqueness. But more than that, I wanted to tell him how strong my Jewishness made me feel. I wanted to tell him how it gave me roots in a way that my blackness could not. Black was nothing more than a color to me. I was a cultural mulatto. Born and raised without the benefit of Watts chop shops, Motown street corners, or deepdown Smithville fishing holes and Chinaberry trees, I was only as black as derision or casual observation would carry. My color was a nuisance. I was too black to be white, too white to be black. For the first few years of my conversion I had a sense of self I'd never known before. And the derision hardly mattered at all.

I talked about myself, but for some reason, didn't say the things I wanted to say, or even tell him the usual lies. I told him that being both black and Jewish wasn't all that interesting or special, that I'd been black for seventeen years, and didn't think of it much, and I'd been a Jew for less than six months, and had a lot to learn. It was all true, but not what I wanted to say. He talked about himself too, but neither of us listened very well, I think. We weren't conversing so much as monologing. Maybe that's why I never told him the usual fibs. Maybe I sensed that the very words we exchanged weren't mutually intelligible. We were so different.

Finally, we reached the little storefront place. The Jesus Bar and Grill or something like that. The place was predictably dismal inside. Dark, naked with a hint of tamari sauce in the air. It was furnished with rickety, mismatched tables and chairs. Clean, but not religiously clean. As if it had been swept by a guy who managed to keep his hands in his pockets while sweeping. Laid back clean. There were only two people in the place, an old, freeze-dried wino with brown teeth and knuckles the size of cue balls, and Jerry, Caspar's friend, and "brother in Christ." "Say, Jer," said Caspar. "Where is everybody?"

A short, dark, long-haired guy slipped from behind the bar and stuck his hairy hand out at me. I shook it and tried to return his gargantuan smile, but it overwhelmed me. The best I could do, as I usually do, was give him a stiff grin.

"His name's Spider," said Caspar. "He's on the team."

"Whoa, far-out name. Nice to meet you, Spider."

"Stuart's his real name, but it sounds too formal and he don't like to be called Stu."

"Far-out, far-out. I can dig it."

"Say, where is everybody?" said Caspar."

"Uh, they're all down at the chapel laying hands on Star, man. Her old boyfriend, Wild Bill, that biker from the Sons? talked her into doing some acid Saturday and she's all convicted now. They oughta be back in a couple of hours." He kept pulling on his hair as he spoke. He had one of the most beautiful heads of hair I'd ever seen. Wavy and full. With his neatly trimmed beard his "resemblance" to Jesus couldn't possibly have gotten by anyone, least of all himself, I figured. With his free hand he beckoned us to the table next to him, turned and smiled at the old wino. "Hey, Pete," he said. "These are a couple of brothers in Christ, Caspar and Skyler. Sit down, brothers." The wino turned from the counter and slobbered something I couldn't catch. "Um, we found Pete sleeping in Monument Park last Friday. We've been trying to dry him up some and help him find work, but he wants us to make him our pastor."

"We don't have a pastor," said Caspar.

"Yeah, I know, um, like I try to tell him we're egalitarian and everything, but he really doesn't understand. He says a church can't exist without a pastor and since he doesn't consider us a church he says he doesn't have to quit drinking. Um, would you guys like some juice?" He stepped behind the bar, still pulling his hair, and came back with three bottles of that weird-tasting juice with all the sediment at the bottom of the bottle. We sat there like a bunch of yutzes, shaking these bottles, while Jerry talked about egalitarianism, how screwed-up the Catholics were, and how "together" the Jews had been before they blew it.

"Say, Jer," said Caspar. "You'll never guess what Spider is."

"OK, man, I give up. What are you, bro?"

"Tight end, I guess," I said. I was being coy. I knew damned well what Caspar was implying.

"No you're not, soul brother. Well, yeah you are, but that's not what I mean."

"What is he? What is he?"

Casper laid a hand on my shoulder and leaned across the table till his face was just inches from Jerry's. "This guy's Jewish," he said.

"Whoaaaaaa."

"Isn't that far-out?"

"Fer suuuure."

They sat there looking at their juice, nodding, saying, "Fer sure. Fer sure." Then Jerry, pulling on his hair a little frantically, said, to no one in particular. "You know, that guy Sammy Davis, Jr.'s Jewish too."

*

It wasn't what you could call love at first sight, but I got used to him. I found I couldn't, as many people had before me, tell him to go take a flying fart. And I guess I'd be a liar if I said I never cared about him. There were a million things I didn't like about him, but he tried so damned hard to be a good friend.

Once I missed the activity bus after football practice because I'd stayed in the whirlpool too long. I'd missed the bus several times before and my father had gotten fed up with having to pick me up all the time. He told me if I missed the bus one more time I could walk home for all he cared. He wasn't joking. If it had been any other night I wouldn't have minded the seven-mile walk, but this night was windy and snowing. I didn't have money for a cab or even a bus, and it's damned near impossible to hitch a ride in Colorado Springs if you're black. Not even black folks will stop for you.

I walked to Caspar's house which was only about a mile and a half from Palmer High. He invited me in for dinner. I told him I couldn't stay, that I'd just like to have one of his folks take me home if possible. He told me his father worked nights and they only had one car. He, his mother, and his sister kept insisting that I sit down and eat with them. After refusing their hospitality for awhile, I sat down with them and immediately they started in on a family debate on the best way to get me home. They finally decided to call a cab for me, but I told them no thanks. Mrs. Rupert kept saying, "Oh nonsense. Oh nonsense." And then by some astonishing twist of logic, started telling me how her sister had died because she had neglected to take care of her bladder infection. "She was only twenty-six, Stuart. Have some more chicken, dear." Caspar kept saying, "Pride goeth before a fall, Spy. Pride goeth before a fall." His sister kept saying, "We can't let him walk in that weather, Mom, let him stay here. Mom, call Dad. Mom, call his parents. You can't go out in weather like this." They all spoke at once and it was all I could do to keep from screaming and running home. Finally, I said:

"I . . . uh appreciate all your concern, but I think my father's trying to teach me a lesson. If I show up in a taxi he might get pretty upset with me. Especially if you pay for it." This shut them all up. Amazingly, none of them ever brought up the fact that it was I who had come to ask for a ride in the first place. After dinner I thanked them and went for my coat. Caspar got up from the table, went to his bedroom and came back with *his* coat. "I'll walk you home, Spy."

"That's OK, Caspar."

"Pride goeth before a fall, Spy."

"It's got nothing to do with pride."

"If a man asketh you to walketh with him one mile, goeth with him two."

"What?"

"It's the Lord's will, my man."

Mrs. Rupert hugged us both as if we were off for the Bloody Somme in 1917. She and Caspar's sister stood at the door and waved to us till we turned the corner. "Oh nonsense," I thought to myself. "Nonsense."

As I said, it was terribly cold out that night; nevertheless, we loped along in the usual high school jock manner. Every so often, Caspar would nudge me and tell a joke. Some of them were funny, some were not. Then he nudged me on the arm, said. "Do you know any Jewish jokes?"

"A few," I said.

"Tell me one. I don't know any."

"Let's see. OK. My friend Dave told me this one a couple of years ago. It's about this guy who'd been Jewish all his life and one day he walks up to his best buddy, Murray, and says to him, 'Murray, guess what. I just converted to Christianity.'

"'What?' says Murray, 'Are you serious?'

"'Yeah, but I want you should do me a favor.'

"'What do you want?' says Murray.

"'I want you should also convert.'

"'Get outta here. You're meshuggah. Why—'"

"What?" said Caspar. "He's what?"

"Meshuggah. It means crazy."

"Is that Jewish?"

"Yeah, but it's called Yiddish."

"How come?"

"Because that's the name of the language, dummy. Do you want me to tell you this joke or not?"

"Go ahead. I just axed a question."

"Well, fine. So anyway the guy says, 'That's crazy—'"

"Mu-sugar."

"Fuck. Never mind."

"Come on, Spy."

"Forget about it. I'll tell you tomorrow."

He kept badgering me, but I wouldn't tell him. We were quiet for awhile. The wind let up, and we were thankful for that, but the snow continued to fall. After awhile, Caspar said, "Jews don't believe in Jesus, do they?"

"Well, it's not like we think he's like Santa Claus or Superman, or something. We just don't think of him as our savior."

"Why not?"

"It's too complicated to explain."

"Can you be a Jew and believe in Jesus?"

"Not hardly."

"What if I converted? I believe in Jesus. What if I converted? Then I'd be a Jew in the Lord."

"You'd be a Jew on the street. No rabbi in the world would

convert you. Listen, a Jew who believes in Jesus is like a Christian who don't. It's just not possible, you dope."

"Lighten up, Spy." He patted my shoulder. "You still hear from your friend Dave?"

"Nope."

"How come?"

"Doesn't have my address."

"How come?"

"Jeez, Cas. What is this, 'Sixty Minutes'? 'How come? How come? How come?'"

"Don't get warped on me, Spy. I ain't asking you if you killed somebody."

"Who's got time to write? I got friends all over the country, not to mention the Philippines and Germany. I can't keep in touch with everybody. Dave understands."

"Yeah, but I thought you guys were best friends."

"We were friends."

"I don't know. Just don't seem right."

"What do mean you don't know. Dave's an air force brat. He understands. Besides, maybe he's moved. Maybe he'd be too busy to write me. Who the hell knows? You sure don't. You don't know what it's like."

"Yeah, but you could at least send him your address. You gotta figure the guy'd like to hear from you. I'd send you my address. What do you got to lose?"

We'd walked about halfway, and I was very tired and irritable. We were silent for awhile. The glow from a car's headlights crept over my shoulder and I turned toward it, poked out my thumb. "Damn, it's cold," I said.

"No way anybody'll pick us up, Spy." He nudged me with the elbow. "Hey, if you move? I'll write you."

"Right."

"Well, I would."

"OK, OK. Hey, Caspar, we're about halfway now. I think you should go back."

"I don't mind."

"I do. In the first place it's getting late, and if you think my Dad's gonna give you a ride home, you're nuts. In the second place, I'm in a pretty bad mood. I want to be by myself. I appreciate you walking all this way with me, but it's not like I asked you to. Don't see why you did it in the first place."

He lowered his head and sighed. "I'll go if you want me to. You're not mad at me, are you?"

"No."

"OK, I'll head back, but you gotta tell me the rest of the joke."

"Jeez—"

"Come on, Spy, be a bud—"

"The guy Murray says, 'You're meshuggah, Why do you want me to convert?'

"'Because,' the guy says. 'I'd like to have at least one Christian friend.'"

"Is that it?"

"That's it."

"I don't get it."

"Yeah, well, it's too hard to explain. Well, take it easy. See you tomorrow."

He said goodnight. I kept walking.

*

The Camel was always protective of me. Always wanted to fight for me whether I needed someone to fight for me or not. He always asked his mother to pack a little something extra in his lunch bag for me. For some reason, they assumed I was poor. Whenever I talked about quitting football, he talked about quitting football. We'd go to a movie: If I hated it, he hated it, even when it was obvious he hadn't. He was lonely and I watched him struggle for my friendship. Sometimes I enjoyed seeing him struggle. I hated myself for that, but I often enjoyed the feeling anyway. I'd hurt him sometimes and he'd ignore me for days. And I couldn't believe it when I found myself struggling for his friendship.

Still, he would bend more than I. It was only his Christian beliefs that he refused to bend one way or another. He constantly witnessed to me. He was always shoving these grotesque little tracts into my gym locker. One day I told him to take his tracts and shove them up his hip pads.

"What's wrong with em?" he said.

"They make me sick, that's what's wrong with em."

"Well, what?"

"Aw man, look at this crap." I grabbed one from my locker and threw it open. "First of all," I said, "these are ugly—"

"Ugly?"

"You're damned right. Ugly. Looks like a third-grader drew em. And listen to this garbage. 'Oh my God . . . where's my wife??? All the REAL Christians are gone! . . . the . . . rapture came, just like she said it would! AAIIEEEEE!' And check this out. This swarthy guy comes up and says, 'The only only force that can stop the movement of *communism* is the gospel of Jesus Christ, but we have no fear of the United States—because in actuality, comrade, it is not a Christian nation and it will not back its *missionaries.*' I mean God. How can you take this shit seriously, Caspar? Do you really believe this mumbo-jumbo?"

"You won't be calling it mumbo-jumbo when the rapture does come and the communists do come."

"Aw Christ—"

"Don't take the name of the Lord in—"

"Christ! Christ! Christ! Christ! I'll give you some vain, chump. I'm Jewish, asshole. If I thought being Christian was worth it I'd be Christian. Quit putting this trash in my locker." Caspar put up his dukes and started ducking and weaving in front of me. "What are you doing?" I said.

"You wanna tag, let's tag."

Before I could decide whether to hit him, Coach Giamadi walked in. "Ruppert. Massey," he said. "What are you scrotums doin?" Camel dropped his arms. "Nothing, coach."

"You two come here to squirrel around or play ball?"

We looked at each other.

"Huh?"

We looked at the floor.

"Fifty pushups, ten laps, and come see me after practice. And don't make me come lookin for you."

We looked at him.

The laps and the pushups were nothing, but when coach made us hug each other in front of the whole team, I wanted to cry. For the rest of the year, and then some, they called us The Honey Boys.

*

Caspar scored our only touchdown in a dismal game against Wasson High. Though we'd been beat by thirty-six points he couldn't even begin to contain his picket-fence grin as we jogged off the field at the final whistle. I was as pissed off as the rest of the guys on the team, but not because of the loss. For the first half of the season I'd played tight end, but couldn't catch so much as a cold. Caspar had played defensive end, but couldn't tackle a corpse. So coach switched our positions.

I hated the idea of his catching my goddamned pass and scoring my goddamned touchdown. In the showers, the boy went nudge crazy, laughing, joking, talking smack. He wasn't popular with most of the guys on the team and nobody seemed terribly pleased that he'd scored the only touchdown. Guys kept reminding him we were a team and because we'd lost, his "Big Six" meant "zilch."

Caspar didn't seem to care. He was thrilled. He invited a few guys to his place for lunch. Nobody accepted but Mike "Big

Stick" Hardy, and I. After a couple of greasy cheeseburgers and about ninety hours of his mother hugging him and his father slapping him on the back and calling him champ, we went to the park and threw a football around. He must have recounted his heroic midfield grab about three hundred times. It would have been bearable if he'd left out the slow motion, and the "Ruppert's at the thirty. He's at the twenty-five. Down to the twenty. The fifteen. The ten. He's gone! He's gone! TOUCH-DOOOWN! Big Caspar Ruppert scores the Big Six!" Made me sick. He got friskier every time I threw him the ball so I told the guys I was bushed. We sat down under a cluster of gigantic pines and made comments on all the girls we saw. Still, whenever he could, the Camel would say something about "The Big Six."

"Hey, Caspar, man, why don't we talk about something else." He looked hurt for a split second and then the usual big grin slid back onto his face. "You guys wanna hear a Jewish joke?" he said. "My lab partner in biology lab told me it."

"Sure," said Big Stick.

"OK," said Caspar. "What's the difference between a Jew and a pizza?"

"Oh Christ. Alright, what's the difference between a Jew and a pizza?" I said.

"Pizzas don't scream when you put em in the oven."

He made the funniest noise when I hit him. It sounded like a small dog's bark. The blood on his shirt made a line of perfect little dots. I felt terrible the moment I'd done it. "Motherfucker," he said. But he didn't say anything more.

"That's no way for a Christian to talk."

"What the fuck you hit me for?"

"Sheeiit."

"It was a joke."

"Why ain't you laughing?"

"Well you never hit me when I tell black jokes."

"I've heard em all before."

"So you'd hit me if you hadn't heard em?"

"You can't tell jokes like that about black people."

"What's the big deal?"

He started crying. Actually crying. I didn't know what to do. The Stick and I took the bus home.

Big Stick and I sat down in the very back of the bus. Neither of us spoke for about the first couple of miles. Then, Big Stick turned to me. "You sure popped him a good one, Spider."

"Yeah."

"What did he say? Was it that joke?"

"No. Guy just gets on my nerves."

"Yeah, mine too, a little. He's not a team player."

The Stick was quiet for awhile and then he said. "But if it wasn't the joke, what did you mean by, 'You can't tell black jokes like that one'?"

I squirmed in my seat. Stick was one of the smartest guys on the team, a second-string quarterback and an honors student. The kind of person who, behind a peach-cheeked, blue-eyed mask, could ask the most penetrating questions without your suspecting a thing. He'd caught me in a lie or two before. I had learned to be wary of him. The thing that bothered me the most about him was that when he'd point out to me the inconsistencies in the things I claimed, he maintained the peachy innocence. He was always kind, forgiving, tolerant. I couldn't stand this. He seemed to like me very much, but I always tried to avoid him. "Well, maybe it was the joke, a little." I said. "I dated a Jewish chick when we lived in Nebraska. Her grandparents were killed by Nazis in World War II. I didn't mean to hit him. It was automatic. I shouldn't have done it."

"Surprised me. I always thought you guys were kind of tight."

"Not really. Guy's never even been to my house."

That was true.

"But you're always together at school."

"He's always around me. He always hangs around me. I hate it when people try to get too close. I'm kind of a loner."

*

After football season I hardly saw the Camel at all. I heard he had started smoking dope. He didn't go out for football the next year and I saw him just every once in awhile at school with some of his friends from the bar and grill. I can't say I missed him all that much. I started hanging out with Mike Hardy and his friends. I went up a notch or two on the popularity meter. I ran for class vice-president and was elected. Caspar started wearing funky headbands and tried to grow a beard. I worked on the yearbook staff and was chosen to attend the annual Urban League dinner as the student representative for the district. Caspar got caught pissing out the cafeteria window and OD'd on reds at the fall bonfire. I broke my right knee all to pieces in a football game. Caspar punched out Coach Giamadi during gym class. Coach had called him a pussy. I went to graduation ceremonies and got a medium-nice round of applause. Caspar went up to Hot Springs and got laid.

Months went by. I was working at Safeway as a stocker. I was considering quitting and working elsewhere. My grades weren't good enough for college. I thought about the military, though the war in Vietnam was still cooking. I didn't think about the Camel. Then one day he called me. I surprised myself. I was actually glad to hear from him.

"Caspar! How the hell are you, dude?"

"Hey, Spy, what's happenin, soul brother?"

"So what's the deal, man?"

"So how's it hangin, man?"

He had an apartment on the west side. I was anxious to get there. Partly because I was looking forward to seeing him, partly because I wanted to see his place. While on the way there, I recalled how we had parted and I grew a little paranoid. I wondered whether he might be setting me up. I tried to tell myself the thought was ridiculous, but he had changed. Almost overnight. By the time I got to his door I couldn't keep my hands from trembling.

It wasn't a bad place at all. It was a basement place, aluminum foil on the ceiling, black lights, day-glo posters of Jimi, Black Sabbath, Conan, and several centerfolds. I wasn't crazy about the decor, but it seemed nice and clean. Caspar sat in the middle of the floor on a bright green, cheap-looking throw rug. He had a guitar across his knees, a Marlboro between two fingers, and a bottle of Boon's Farm apricot wine in front of him.

"Hiya, Spy, ya big guy."

He didn't look happy, but he seemed glad to see me. My apprehension subsided. "What's up, hippy?" I said.

"The sky."

He offered me some wine. I took a couple of swigs.

"Just don't nigger-lip it."

"Look who's talking. This homely white boy with Firestone stamped on his lips." We laughed at this piss-poor icebreaker and went back to asking so-how's-it-going type questions for a little while. I hadn't liked his nigger-lip remark any more than he liked my Firestone thing. I've always hated that, yuck-yuck-yuck-we're-just-a-couple-of-liberal-minded-buddies-who-can-call-each-other-racist-names-and-not-even-flinch-cause-we're-really-above-all-that bullshit. Makes me sick.

When the stiff greetings were over, Caspar crushed his cigarette out in an ashtray, let out a long sigh and ran his fingers through his hair. "You OK?" I said. He sighed again.

"I don't know, man, I don't know."

"So cry on my shoulder, Shirley."

"Know why I'm living here?"

"Cause you pay rent?"

"C'mon, Spy."

"Sorry."

"My dad threw me out."

"Wow."

"Yeah, well you know all that shit I pulled in school. I don't know what happened, I . . . Dad, he just . . . well, he just kept asking me to straighten up and be like you. He kept asking why I wasn't more like you. I mean, all the time it was Stuart this and Stuart that. No offense, man, but I don't need that . . . well . . . "

"Phony?"

"Naw . . . yeah. Yeah, that shit's phony. But you know what hurt me the most, Spy? Like he never said, 'Hey, Caspar, why don't you go back to being like you were?' He never said that. It was always you he was asking me to be like." He took a sip of wine, pulled at his hair a couple of times as I had seen his friend Jerry do. "Mom made him help me get a job at Hewlett Packard before he kicked me out. My chick was here for awhile, but she split back home. You ever meet her?"

"I saw you guys together at school a couple of times. Nice chick."

She wasn't.

"Why'd she leave?"

"Got sick of me. Why did you leave?"

He downed some wine, passed me the bottle.

"I'm not sure why we couldn't get along, Caspar. I really don't—"

"I know you don't. But I know why."

He paused, obviously wanting me to ask him why, but I was afraid. We sat there, silent for maybe five minutes. His face looked ugly under that purple light. His complexion had gotten worse. I sifted my mind for something to break the silence, maybe even cheer things up. But I didn't want to ask him the question. He looked up, but not at me. He seemed to be staring through the Conan poster, through the wall, deep into the earth. "Stuart," he said after a long time staring.

He called me Stuart.

"Hmmm?"

"I *was* like you. I was a lot like you. But it was weird, the more like you I got the less like you I was. There was always stuff I knew you were thinking and feeling that you never admitted to. Every time I thought I knew you better, you kind of disappeared." He paused to light a cigarette. "The main thing about you, Spy, is you're a bastard. You were waiting the whole time to hit me. All I had to do was say the wrong thing, which was for you, the right thing."

"That's not true."

"So then why didn't you just tell me it was wrong instead of hitting me? We're supposed to be friends. What does it matter what your religion is if you don't take the time to tell people what it's about? You and me *are* friends. Maybe not best friends anymore, but we are friends. You should have explained to me about that joke."

"But we're so different, Cas. I figured—"

"*You're* different. You're the one who's different. OK, so you're the differentest black guy in the world and nobody can be like you, or figure you out. Nobody can jack you around. B.F.D., man. The point is you're my friend, Spider. Friend. It's just like religion. It just takes faith. That's all there is to it."

I couldn't stay. I couldn't sit there and listen to him. I couldn't touch him. I couldn't say anything. I couldn't do anything. Almost on the verge of feeling, I hovered somewhere in my mind and, for some reason, thought about Brother Sammy Davis, Jr., standing in front of an endless white audience singing "That Old Black Magic." I couldn't even move.

How I Met Idi at the Bassi Dakaru Restaurant

IT was my sixth day in Senegal and I'd just made up my mind to grab a quick breakfast, run over to the travel agency, and make reservations for a trip to some place like Freetown, Georgetown, or Kano. I'd grown weary of miscommunicating in Berlitz Babyfrench. I'd been cheated at markets, scammed in hotels, flaked in restaurants. I was lonely, dazed, and flat-brained. Couldn't conjure one reason to stay.

Senegal, particularly Dakar, is the most discombobulating place I know. Even today, six years after my return to the United States and a semifrustrating semirewarding, unwaveringly quotidian life as an anthropology teacher at a private school in Denver, I still can't unscramble the experience. I still can't make whohow from wherewhat. But if it hadn't been for Idi, I would have spied Madame Senegal from a distance, like a lone hunter spies a pride of hungry lions, turned on my heel, and skulked away.

So that morning I stepped into the Bassi Dakaru restaurant for my farewell breakfast. The first thing that hit me was the smell of the place. It had a sweet-sour-decaying, vaguely homey smell, and I immediately lost my appetite. The restaurant was nice to look at, as far as dollar-a-meal chop shops go. Rather than leave, I decided to stay, have something to drink, and enjoy the atmosphere. Multi-colored flystrips hung in the windows, impotent, but pretty. There were slender, green bottles sitting on each table. I suspected they were for candles, but there were no candles in them. Next to each bottle sat two saucers, one for pepper, one for salt. The tables themselves were beautiful, a heavy wicker done in natural finish. All of them were unoccupied except for one in the middle of the room. At it sat two men, one young, one rather old. I sat a respectable distance from them and watched them eat their breakfast—white bread, and bitter-smelling coffee. I could hear their sipping from where I sat. They seemed to be enjoying their racket, sitting luxuriously in their chairs, rolling their heads back at each sip like watering herons. I watched them for several minutes. I knew I was being impolite, but at this early stage in my journey, I fell intrigued by the fluidity of African movement. Africans don't walk. They roll; they glide.

One of them, the older fellow, looked up at me. My heart bounded. Oh, Christ, I thought. He's pissed, I can tell. I pretended to be looking for a waiter. The old man smiled, stood and approached me. My heart pounded in my temples as I stood to shake his hand. "You want some chop?" he said. "I'm from the States," I said. He cocked his head, shook my hand, said, "Idi, my cousin, he have very good English, very fine." He then summoned his cousin, a young man of twenty-five or so, handsome-ugly, flat, quick eyes, thin face, coffee bean black, worker's arms, firm grip. "What you know good, man?" said Idi. It took me a while to figure out what he'd said to me. The words were clear enough, but his emphasis was peculiar. Instead of sounding like, "Whaccha know *good* man," it sounded like, "Whod due *know* good, mahn."

"Breakfast, I guess," I said.

Of course he laughed, and subjected me to the usual torture of listening to my fumble in translation. After Idi and his cousin checked their laughter, Idi introduced me to his cousin, Kene, chief cook, head waiter, and major stockholder of the Bassi Dakaru Restaurant. I also learned that the two were originally from Bassi Santa Su, Gambia, but came to Dakar just prior to the Gambian Coup in eighty-one.

Kene and I sat down; Idi remained standing. "What do you eat for breakfast?" he said.

"Just some tea, please, and maybe a roll, if you've got one."

"No problem. I will be right back." He spun round and glided toward the counter/kitchen area. Kene wiped his brow on the sleeve of his boubou, sipped the hell out of his coffee. "It is too hot this day, you think?" he said. I agreed, but could think of nothing else to say. Then after a minute or so, I said, "Where I'm from it never gets this hot." Kene asked me where I was from and in the same sentence, more or less, asked me whether I was in the Peace Corps. It ran something like: "Where from did the Peace Corps did he have send you?"

"I'm an anthropologist. I'm here to study African literature. I'm here to study the griot, and collect folktales and such. See, I want to find a connection between . . . " The old man looked at me in the same way I'd have looked at him if he'd spoken to me in full-tilt Wolof, so I clammed up. "I'm from Colorado," I said. Idi returned with my order. He slid a bowl of toast in front of me and half a dozen flies made it room and board before I could touch it. Idi poured my tea and handed me a spoon. "Do you do well in this business, Kene?" I asked. He grunted, scratched his head, yawned, and said, "I see many rainy season, and many dry season too, but with no Idi, I have no business any." He gave Idi a quick look. Idi didn't respond, but I sensed some sort of uneasiness develop between the two. Idi lowered his slender face, finally, and looked at his uncle. I couldn't read his face. He cleared his throat and said, "That was a long time ago. I had a different name then."

A different name? I thought. Maybe he's some kind of hustler. Maybe these guys are setting up a joke. Maybe I misunderstood him. What does he mean by different name? With considerable effort I kept my trap shut. I squirmed in my chair and fiddled with my toast. The restaurant grew warmer, flies swirled about. I watched Kene as he grinned at his cousin. "Idrissa," he said, "say this young boy how you take Bassi Dakaru for ourself from the whiteman."

"That's OK," I blurted. "He doesn't have to."

"Oh, no, no, no, is OK for him." And then he spoke in

Wolof to Idi for two or three minutes. Then, "You say him, Idi. You say him."

"I will get some kola first," said Idi. He left the table and went behind the counter, returning with three kola nuts, three less than spotless glasses, and three bottles of beer. He broke open one of the kolas and gave me half. It was bitter as an apple seed, not at all what I'd expected, and I made a face. The two men smiled, but didn't laugh. They each took a portion of kola, then Idi filled our glasses. They saluted me, and drank. Kene finished his beer in one blast, then refilled his glass. Idi sipped and cleared his throat.

"When a young boy in my village in Gambia, the people used to call me Leuk-Idrissa because I would trick everybody and make a lot of practical jokes on them. Leuk is the name of the rabbit in children's stories who tricks everyone, you see."

I told him I was familiar with many of the characters from African folktales.

"Every day," said Idi, "everybody in my village would be shaking their fist at me and crying in a loud voice, 'Leuk-Idi is too much trouble and very soon we will kick him out of the entire village!'

"I would laugh at this, of course, because no one in my village could throw me out because could I always trick them. I had very powerful *tere. Tere* is the true Wolof word for gris gris, which I don't know what it means. In Wolof, *tere* means book because the power in it comes from the Koran.

"One morning, when I was in my bed sleeping, two policemen came and arrest me with handcuffs and mace. 'Hey,' I say to these polices, 'what are you doing?' I say this to them because I never saw a police in our village before, and also I could not think what I did against these men. They put on me the handcuffs and a blindfolds, threw me in a wagon, and took me to jail where they charge me with taking Mrs. M'baye's goat which I did not do at all. I stay in prison for three years and a few days. It was very bad there. Every day they try to beat me and try to kill me. One time they did not give me any food and water for sixty-four days, but I would trick rodents to eat. Another time they shoot me with guns, but I trick the bullets away from me. When I left there, I had a very bad attitude about all this police business."

Idi told this story with a matter-of-factness incongruent to its content. I knew he was greening me, but I couldn't tell whether he knew I knew. Does he think I'm stupid? Or am I missing some subtle allegory? Is he schizophrenic? I suppressed any outward sign of disbelief and listened to Idi.

"I left there by tricking as usual. I trick a guard into forgetting what means 'open' and what means 'close,' and when night came I walk out of the prison and never return there."

Kene opened another kola and refilled our glasses. I sat chewing my piece of kola, oblivious to its bitterness. I told myself it didn't matter whether these guys were pulling my leg. Idi was a terrific storyteller. Though his story was a dozen clicks left of believable, he told it without the disgusting archness of an Uncle Remus, Burl Ives, or Mark Twain. Those guys with unctuous grins, twinkly eyes, and winks. He told his story with a simple clarity, as if he were telling the truth. Maybe he was. He told me about some of his adventures subsequent to his escape, such as tricking a policeman into eating a bowl of termites disguised to look like rice. The man was "devoured inside to outside." He told me of his adventures in a bush full of horrifying creatures, and a city full of horrifying concepts. He told me about his return to his village on the wind of a Sufi's sneeze. "Some people don't believe what the Sufis can do," he said. He told it all without crinkling his nose, winking, whipping out a corncob pipe, or asking dopey questions like, "So what do you think I did next?" The beer, the kola, the story made me lose track of time. I forgot about the travel agent and the tab I was running up, and found myself almost believing him.

"I was too hungry and thirsty because the whole time I was in the bush I could not find food to eat but dead insects and no water except for the rain. When I return to my village, I went to my house to eat any possible food there, but there was none. So I went to my mother's house to eat her food, but when I got there I saw there was no food, but the whiteman had it all. That is what my mother say to me.

"I walk from house to house in my village and saw that everyone had no food but only the whiteman had it. I went to the whiteman's house which was a store and a church too. I was shock when I see him for I had never seen a whiteman before. He had a white face and hands. His feet were black, but like beetles and not like feet. I ask the whiteman for food but he say to me I need money to have food from him. I gave him cowries but he laugh only and say not cowries can buy food anymore, only money from white people's houses which, at this time, you could only find on the other side of the world.

"He wouldn't give. Even I could not trick away from him food because, in those days, the whitemen were too smart to trick. I went from his store thinking how could I get from him his store or get a store of my own, but I did not find out. The people of my village were starving. They ate only a little food because the whiteman had it all, and the whiteman said only people with license could fish in the streams, but the license was too expensive for my people. I decide to build my own store without food and trade it for the whiteman's store which had food. I build my store in a year and two weeks and then asked the whiteman to trade with me. He laugh like Golo the monkey only and say to me that no black man can build a store to trade with a whiteman because the black man did not know the secret of running water which all stores need to be official.

"I went to the bush the next day and took with me my most powerful tricking *tere.* I went to River to ask him to follow me home to go in my faucets, but he say to me, 'No.' So I went to find Rat and say to him that his cousin's house is burning down. 'But what must I do?' he cry to me. And I say he must bring water to his cousin's house which is in my village.

"'But how do I do this?' he say.

"'You must dig through the bottom of River and go to my store in the village.' I gave to Rat a map to follow which lead exactly to the faucets in my store, and he did as I say.

"Then I went to the whiteman's store to make my trade with him. When I show him the faucet he was frighten for a moment, but then he laugh and speak like this: 'You still do not have a store as fine or official as mine as you do not know the secret of whiteman's windows.'"

It was getting late in the day. Idi told his story with serene ease. The beer was in my veins, now, and my anthropological objectivity flowed away. Kene sat with us as much as he could, but very often, busied himself with customers who had begun to steadily stream in at about 1:00 P.M. He graciously greeted them, made polite small talk. I could tell he was proud of his place, and that he took good care of his customers. Though the restaurant buzzed with voices, though glasses and spoons and plates clanked and plinked, I was deep in Idi's world.

". . . and so I rode on Buzzard's back up to Sky, and I say to Sky that I don't want to make trouble, but I hear from Golo that Earth believe it is himself who should be on above and you who should be below. And when Sky hear this his whole face turn black, black, black, and he say. 'He is crazy! How could this be? Only Allah can put Earth over Sky or Sky over Earth. I have never heard of anything like this in my life. What about the rain? Does Earth think that rain can fall up? Does he think he can clean the clouds and birds with pebbles and sand? Wyyo! He is a foolish man, this Earth.'

"So Sky threw down a lightning at the sand on the beach and melt the sand to glass. And when the glass became cold, I took it home and polish it until it was a perfect window. When the white man saw what I did, he scream on the top of his lungs and he say, 'No, no, no! This is not possible for a black man to do! But if you think you are so smart, you will see what happen when you try to make a refrigerator. This, you cannot do.'

"Well, this was very easy, and this was very hard, because even though I could build the refrigerator box from Elephant's tusks, I could not find out how to make it cold. This had me very worry because every day I witness me and my people starving from hunger. Many of my people died, and we had to bury them in the ground. One day I was digging a hole in the ground, and I notice that the ground was cold. So I dig deeper into the ground to find out where was this curious cold from. I dig down, down, down until I find a house where all my dead relatives were living. 'Hey,' I say to my cousin Penda, 'why is it so cold in here?' She said, 'It is cold because Death is cold, and this house belongs to Death.' Then I had this idea to talk to Death and get from him the secret of cold to put in my refrigerator. It was very difficult to find this Death because his house was bigger than all of Senegal. I walked for days and days. But finally I found his room, which was the size of Dakar. I knock on his door and when he spoke the sound shook the inside of my bones. 'Who dare to knock on my door?' he say. But I did not tell him my name, but I say like this: 'I am a whiteman name Jack Marlboro and my refrigerator has lost all its cold. I need some more for it.' Death say nothing for awhile, and then he say, 'Come in so we can make the arrangements.' But I did not come in. I say to him that I must return to my store to starve more customers so that he himself could have more dead people. But Death say that he could not give me the cold to take back because if he did this I would freeze myself and would have to stay in his house forever. 'Come in my room,' he say, 'so we can make a plan.'

"Before I could think of something to say, his giant door began to open, open, open, but I put myself behind it to hide from him. He walk out of the room, and he was huge. His hands and face were as white as fish bones, and his boubou was made from human skin. He had deep red eyes that were caves, and his teeth were long spears. He turn left and right but I was behind him, and he could not see me. 'But I can't see you, Jack Marlboro. Where are you? Come in my room and we will have tea and discuss this refrigerator," he say. When he step away from the door to find me, I ran into his room and close the door to his back. 'Hey!' he say, 'Let me in my own room!' But I say to him I cannot do this unless he give me the cold that I want from him. 'Fine,' say Death to me. 'Come outside and I will give you cold.' I said this is OK with me on one condition, I say to him that if I find someone else to carry the cold for me then he cannot harm me. Death consider this for a long time, but later he say to me, 'OK.'

"Then I remove my boubou and my sandals. I next ran to his closet and remove one of his boubous from it. Since his clothes were made from human skin, I think you can see what my plan was. I cut his clothes to look like a person and then fill the pattern with the straw in his mattress. Then I put my boubou on this puppet I made and sat him down in a chair.

"When I open the door, Death came back into his room and reach out his hand to touch me, but I say to him, 'But you made a bargain with me and you cannot touch me.' Death laugh at me like a barking dog and say to me. 'You're a stupid man. How you expect this puppet to carry this cold. It cannot walk—'

"'Just a minute,' I interrupt him, 'This is true he cannot walk, so he will carry the cold and I will carry him.'"

And this is how Idi's story went. The white man would send him off into the wilds to conquer increasingly greater and more complex mysteries of Western technology, and Idi would knock them flat. I could have listened to him till morning. I was quite drunk, but the story and the occasional kola nut kept my mind alert.

Soon the restaurant began to empty, and the air became cooler. Kene sat in the rear of the restaurant counting his day's take. Idi continued.

" . . . so I was in the stomach of the great electrical eel whose inside was made of wires, plugs, switches, and bulbs. I yell to him to let me out, but he say to me he was hungry and, therefore, could not let me go. 'You are my meal,' he said.

"Very soon, I notice that I had to go to the bathroom, but there was no place to relieve myself. I had no idea that this beast did not enjoy water inside him, but only outside him, but I had no place else to go. When I began to pee, the beast told me to stop, but it was too late. Then he short-circuit and die with smoke and fire inside him. I took my knife and collect his many parts. Next I took them to my store and put them in their proper places.

"When the whiteman saw this he pull out all his hairs and ran from the store and gave me the keys to it. Since I did not really want a store, but food only, I gave the keys to my cousin and ate a huge meal."

Idi grinned at me, said, "And Kene made the store into a restaurant so that he could share the food with our people. The Bassi was the first restaurant in my village in Gambia."

Idi and Kene helped me to my feet, and practically carried me to the door. Kene suggested I take a cab home, then stepped to the curb to hail one for me. The night was nearly as warm as the afternoon had been and I really felt like walking. I said so to Idi, but neither he nor his cousin would hear of it. Eventually, a cab pulled up. The two men, with the cabbie's aid, deposited me into the backseat. I asked the cabbie not to pull off until I could say good night to my friends. "Hey, Idi," I said. "You know, at first I didn't know what the hell was going on when you started telling me the story, but now I get you. You told me the story because your cousin told you I collect them, right? That's what you guys were talking about when you were speaking Wolof awhile back, wasn't it?"

"No," said Idi, giving me a quizzical look.

"No? Didn't he tell you I'm here collecting African folktales and all that."

"No, he didn't say that."

"He didn't tell—aw c'mon, blood. If he didn't tell you that, then what were you guys talking about?"

Idi knelt on the sidewalk, rested an elbow on the window

frame of the cab, a grin spread across his face, making it look like a dark planet with two glowing moons and a great smiling ring around it. Then, in a low voice, he said, "He say to me don't leave out the part when I get the giant fly's head for the door-knobs of my store."

"Giant fly? I'm sorry, Idi. I don't recall anything about flies or doorknobs in your story."

"Left it out," said my new friend. "I did not want you to think my story was untrue." He laughed a little, patted my shoulder and stood up. The cabbie threw the car into gear, and I flopped back against the seat, grinning. I closed my eyes and slept all the way back to the Massatta Samb Hotel, my home for nearly six months thereafter.

Rebirth

TREADWELL had not seen a lynching for many years. The souvenirs his father and uncles had deftly sliced from the charred bodies of those black men had long ago disintegrated in the jars of vinegar in which they had been stored. He had thought they would last forever, but as he grew older, he learned that nothing lasts forever. Everything disintegrates, no matter how permanent it seems. At some lynchings, all the flesh would burn to smoking ash, and the only suitable souvenirs the men could collect were blackened teeth and bone fragments. His Uncle Pres had given him a gold-filled molar once, but he hadn't taken care of it and it split into a dozen pieces, leaving only the gold filling. The filling became part of the wedding band he had paid a jeweler to make for his first wife. But she left him after fourteen bad, fruitless years, and he never saw the band again.

As his old truck rumbled its way toward his home, he felt a bottomless melancholy for the days when his arms and legs were as tough as rubber-coated cable, and he could hold onto things, hold them tight, hold them down. But in the last several years he could scarcely hold a coffee cup, a razor, or a screwdriver steady, his hands trembled so. And he felt odd shiftings around in his bones. Sometimes they were painful; sometimes there was no pain at all, just unnervingly silent popping and groaning, like stepping on ripe chinaberries in autumn. He felt, at times, as though his body were floating, naked and senseless, in a vinegar jar. His hair soaking to a dead silver-white, his eyes so paled over they couldn't keep focus on the color and shape of things, his ears turning all sound into a muted hiss.

And his mind worked so strangely these days. Sometimes it did him no more good than a seventy-year-old souvenir jar swirling with fragments of what was once whole. Past, present, and desire, all cast about in orbiting flakes. His head would hurt something awful and his bottom lip would tremble as his mind's eye would strain to focus on some single, unwavering image. He would try to hold onto it as if it were a lifesaver, hoping it would carry him to some place firm and dry. Most usually it was the memory of the last lynching he had seen that pulled things back into a whole again. It was so real: the pink and yellow flames, the stink of gasoline and cooking flesh, his heart drubbing big and loud in his temples. He would hold onto that image and pretty soon all the other images, all the other things he had seen, felt, tasted, understood, would settle into place. His head wouldn't hurt so. His lip wouldn't tremble.

He wondered why and how things had changed so. Why younger men like Myron, who claimed to hate blacks no less than he, seemed almost revolted by the idea of a lynching. "Where in hell-fire," he thought, "have all the men gone?" His stomach knotted at the thought of the conversation he had had with Myron today. "That no good niggerlovin punk," he said to himself, "I got a good mind to . . . " He suppressed the thought, fearing that, as worked up as he was, he might turn the truck around, fly back to the store, and kick the living hell out the boy. Myron would never help him lynch Tossie Green. Never in ten million years. He scrutinized the young man's scrawny frame in his mind's eye. "What kind a so-called men are they makin these days? Hell God damnation, you'd think these boys would look forward to a good ol nigger hangin with good ol fried chicken, lemonade and beer cold enough to crack your teeth, and enough potato salad to choke a horse on. Boy, that's a git together."

Treadwell watched the road with his gray, unblinking eyes.

He smiled as he imagined how Tossie Green would writhe on that rope as fat flames chewed at the soles of his feet. He would struggle like a channel cat on twenty-pound test line. Blisters would swell, pop open and spew hot grease. The nigger would leap, holler, and die. "Boy, that's a git together."

His wife, LouEllen, who had been quietly sitting for the entire ride, turned toward her husband, and cleared her throat as if preparing to sing a hymn. This, he knew, meant that she was preparing to lecture him on his lack of attention toward some trifling domestic chore, or his frequent backsliding from church. He squeezed the wheel and clenched his jaw in anticipation of LouEllen's mindless twaddle. "I don't suppose," LouEllen began, "that you've noticed that Maggie's having this child after only seven months carrying it." Treadwell kept his eyes on the road and said nothing. He felt LouEllen's stare sear the right side of his neck. "Can't say I have," he said after awhile. Then he said to himself, "Lord have mercy, woman, git it over with." The long silences always made him wish LouEllen would disappear. "Wisht you would go off to wherever your voice went off to," he often said to himself. "Or take your fat ass back to that niggerlovin bastard you divorced yourself from."

"I didn't think you would," said LouEllen. "You never give half a mind to the condition of that poor girl. Just work her to death. Poor thing. It's a miracle the poor child never miscarried."

"Well I didn't have no idea she was even like that when I hit er."

"Like what?"

"You know what I mean."

"Pregnant?"

"Now, LouEllen, for cryin out loud—"

"I'm not a bit surprised you didn't have *any* idea what Maggie's condition was. Why you don't even look at the poor thing."

Treadwell grinned inwardly. "No," he said, "but I watch er." He turned toward his wife. The truck swerved. "Are you trying to kill us, Mr. Treadwell?" said LouEllen. "What do you mean you watch her?"

"I mean what I mean."

"Theodore Treadwell, how many times do I have to tell you that that girl does not steal. She's one of the most honest colored in the State of Alabama. In the world maybe. And to tell you the truth, I'm surprised she doesn't steal with what you pay her. You just remember that the next time you go to raising your hand . . . " Treadwell gave a vicious tug to the wheel and slammed on the brakes.

"She's a nigger woman, LouEllen," he hissed, "a nigger woman—and she should a never called me an old fool. Maybe I'm gettin old, but I ain't *no* nigger's fool. In my day . . . " He paused as if searching for the right words. The smell of the old truck, hot oil and gas, rose to his nostrils. Neither he nor his wife moved or spoke for what seemed to be too long a time. He wished that neither he nor his wife nor the world would ever move again. That time would not move beyond 6:53, December 13, 1965. Just stop. Here—right now. That the old truck and his old bones would be covered by dust and pebble and rock. Cover it all up. Bury it. For it made no sense. Maggie had never complained before. Never a peep out those pecan smooth, pecan brown lips. And he had certainly done worse, it seemed to him. Why now? Why all this excitement over a knuckle or two upside the head? Hadn't he done much worse?

LouEllen's voice eased into his consciousness like a telephone ring jangling from a closed room. "It was Clara called you an old fool, Treadwell. How many times do I have to tell—"

"Why you defendin that nigger? I heard what I heard."

"Well then you heard wrong. It was your own daughter called you an old fool, Teddy . . . and the thing that mystifies your daughter and me is—"

"*Step*daughter. Clara's my stepdaughter."

"—is that it was Tuesday when you and Clara had that argument, and Wednesday when you hit Maggie. You just popped out of your chair and liked to knock that child across the kitchen."

"She—"

"I was there, Treadwell, so don't even try to contradict me. Maggie didn't say one mumbling word. I swear, it's like you were just itching for any old reason to hit the girl. The only thing is, you didn't have one. Not a one. What in the Lord's name's wrong with you? And please get this truck to home. We haven't got all day."

But Treadwell merely sat there, gripping the wheel, glaring down the road. His head tightened. He swallowed hard and opened his mouth to speak, but his bottom lip trembled so, he feared his words would sound more peevish than manly. LouEllen tapped his arm. "Sitting *here* won't get us *there*, Treadwell." She sat back, folding her arms, then said, "Don't you forget what her Tossie said to you today. My Grace. My Grace. That boy came out to the house looking to shake your brains loose.

"You—you had better thank your lucky stars you went to work early. Why, if it hadn't been for Clara and me to calm him down he'd have gone out to the store looking for your blood instead of just the tongue-lashing he gave you. And Maggie! Maggie, the girl you knocked down with the back of your hand, begged Tossie not to do anything. The child's black as the devil, but she's near a saint." Her voice raised a notch or two. "Oh yes, Mr. Treadwell, you had better thank your lucky stars." Treadwell started the engine and eased the ancient truck back onto the pavement. "And you, woman," he thought, "better thank your goddamn stars I'm drivin . . . or I'd be wringin your fat neck."

They arrived home as the sky was congealing into a sharp, cobalt blue. The magnolia blossoms that lined the driveway made the air smell citrusy. As Treadwell shut off the engine, the sound of bleating crickets soothed his ears. They stepped through the front door of the house. Treadwell sniffed the warm odor of home and was disappointed to find that supper had not yet been started.

They moved toward the open door of the bedroom. Maggie, lying under a cotton sheet, perspired profusely. Clara leaned over her, applying cool cloths to Maggie's face. The time drew near. Maggie's breathing was irregular and coarse, as she moaned under the blossoming pressure.

"How is she, Clara?" said LouEllen, wringing her hands. She moved closer to the bed. "Just fine, Mama, but it looks to me she's dilated full and Doctor David ain't come yet. He ain't even returned your call. I don't think he's gonna make it in time."

Treadwell hovered in the doorway for a moment, then stepped toward the bed. "Well," he said, "why didn't ya'll just run her over to the dadburn hospital—" LouEllen spun round and pushed him out the room. "Get on out of here, now. It was too late for the hospital when I came out to get you. Water's broke, contractions aren't but a couple of minutes apart—Good Lord, I haven't got time to explain everything to you. This is no place for a man. Get."

"Well, what in damnation you yank me out here for if this ain't—"

"You're here to keep Tossie company in the kitchen. The poor boy's as nervous as a pup in a hailstorm. He needs someone to talk to—"

"Why didn't you get one a his nigger friends to come out here?"

"Go on. Clara and I have work to do."

"Well, why?"

"Cause none of them ever hit his gal, and none of them owes him an apology. . . . And I just can't see you sitting up in that store making money for yourself after what you did to his gal."

"What! What did she say? What do you mean?"

"Tossie's waiting, Mr. Treadwell."

"Stuff Tossie. I ain't never apologized to no nigger in my life. Whud that girl—"

"The kitchen, Theodore." LouEllen shut the door in his face. He backed away from the door. He went first to the bathroom, passed a trickle of water, smoothed his silver crew cut with his palm. He went back to the bedroom door and listened to the low moaning of the black woman and the cooing of his wife and stepdaughter. He turned from the door and headed for the kitchen. "Damn woman," he mumbled. "Goddamn woman."

*

Big Tossie Green gave Treadwell a hard, moonlight stare as the old man timidly slid into the kitchen.

"Well, hello, Tossie."

"Mr. Treadwell."

They offered one another limp hands, shook, neither man looking into the other's eyes. Treadwell imagined a fat rope around Tossie's neck. "Coffee, Tossie?" he said.

"No, thank you."

A mosquito lit on Tossie's arm. He let it stay there.

"Uh, well now, how's the mechanic business comin along, boy?" said Treadwell.

Tossie's neck muscles drew taut. "Just fine," he said.

"Good. Good."

Treadwell smiled too broadly. He felt foolish, and pulled his face into an impassive frown. "Say, uh, Tossie. I hope there's no hard feelins tween you and me after this mornin. I mean, well, I give what I done a lot of thought. A whole lot. An well, you know how it is. Hell. A ol coot like me, well, he don't take to new things so quick. Just can't seem to break these ol timey habits a mine. See what I'm sayin, Toss?"

Tossie slowly rubbed the arm the mosquito had bitten. "Um-hm," he said after a while, "I see what you sayin."

Treadwell watched Tossie's face for a moment, nodded and continued.

"Sometimes, Tossie, sometimes, you see . . . a ol son-of-a-bitch like me, well, he just gits used to things bein a pa'ticaler way. Things just seem to run a whole lot smoother when they run . . . well, when they run the way we're all used to. You followin me, Toss?"

Tossie made no reply.

"Now," said Treadwell. "Now you take that ol truck I got out yonder."

He thumbed back toward the front door.

"Now, I've had that bucket a bolts for goin on twenty-one years, an let me tell you, Tossie, can't nobody make her run like I can. Why, I keep her tuned and oiled an all. I treat her real good, son. Real good.

"Hell, Tossie, I know that ol machine out there better'n the mechanics and engineers what threw er together. I know er, see. An when she gits a little too temper'mental and won't do right no matter how I pets an pampers her, well then, see, I git me a good-size pipe wrench and give it to er good. Why, I just whang the livin daylights out er till she straightens up. An I tell you it ain't failed me yet."

He snatched at a mosquito that had been flying around his head. He thought he had caught it and squeezed long and hard till his knuckles turned white as teeth. He opened his hand and found it empty. He then looked at Tossie who kept his stern gaze on the red checkered table cloth. "But I'm the onliest one can do that, Tossie, cause I been tendin to that ol six-banger for twenty-one years. Can't nobody git good mileage out er like I can. An don't you think for a minute I'd do anything to hurt her. You know what I mean. No real damage. No siree, son. I got just the right touch.

"So you see, Tossie? I mean, you understand, don't you? I mean, mechanickin up in these parts as long as you have an' all. Some things work so good for some folks cause they got em a system slicker'n owl shit. Then the gover'ment or some fellers in fancy suits who don't know nothin about our lives out here comes along an says, Say, fellers, you can't do that no more accordin to code three-of-such-an-such. Hell goddamnation, Tossie, a feller can't make heads or tails out a things no more." He felt himself become a little queasy. "I—I'm sorry, Tossie. Things ain't the way I thought they was supposed to be, son. I'm clean sorry for whuppin your gal."

Silence. And then Tossie lifted a sinewy hand from the table and uncurled one finger and held it just inches from Treadwell's nose. "Let's just hope, Mr. Treadwell . . . . Let's just you and me hope an pray my woman or my child don't die, or your own family gonna go through some changes too. Cause I'm here to tell you right now. I don't give a good gotdamn what the law do to me. I'll break your sorry ass in two just as sure as I'm sittin here."

Tossie lowered his hand. "Just as sure as I'm sittin here. Just like I told you this afternoon."

Silence resumed and hung about them for several long moments. The two men sat together in the sticky heat, moving only to fend off mosquitoes. A bitter bile collected in Treadwell's throat. A thin coat of perspiration bled from his forehead. His mouth felt dry. Never—never in all his sixty-nine years had he ever stooped to a black man. His queasiness grew as he considered the sorrowful state the world had fallen into.

He thought about how utterly frightened he had been this afternoon when Tossie's enormous shadow spilled through the door of Treadwell's General Store. He had lost any will to speak or even to shudder as Tossie hollered, pounded the counter, made astounding threats. It was only when Tossie left that he found his tongue. "Niggers . . . niggers," he croaked while reaching for the oily, blue handkerchief in his back pocket. "I hate them goddamn bastards, Myron." He wiped Tossie's still-warm spittle and his own perspiration from his face. He stared at the doorway through which Tossie had just walked, as if he could summon him back with his steel gray eyes. "I hate em, Myron. You hear me, boy?"

"Sure do, Mr. Treadwell."

"Who in hell-fire do they think they are all of a goddamn sudden? Did you hear what that nigger said to me? Did you *hear* what that . . . never. No nigger never storms in here like a regular man pointin no two-tone finger in my face. Never!"

"Well now, Mr. Treadwell, times have changed, ain't they?"

"Times are supposed to change. Coons ain't. That big black buck stormin in here like a white man an' demandin I don't hit his bitch. You ever see anything like that, boy?"

"Well, it was mighty uppity for a nigger, I got to admit, but . . ."

"But what?" Treadwell began pacing the dusty hardwood floor. Flies buzzed in the hot air and he swung at them. He turned in time to see Myron's face contort in an ugly yawn. "But what, boy?"

"Mr. Treadwell, that gal a Tossie's is . . . well, she's expectin."

"That is beside the point, boy. Who's workin for who?"

"Oh, sir, I'm workin for you, but—"

"I'm talkin about Maggie, stupid. *She* works for *me*, right?"

"Been your housekeeper for damn near eight years, Mr. Treadwell."

"Well then, I got the right to knock hell out er ever now an then, don't I?" He paced as if caged. Sweat trickled down his rippled brow, he wiped it angrily into his crew cut. A fly landed on his hand. He cussed and swung. "Don't I?"

"Well, sir," said Myron, yawning again, "you never hit on me none." A cool breeze wafted in and Myron closed his eyes, leaned back in his chair. The breeze died off in midsentence and the air in the tiny store became instantly hot again.

"I never hit on you, son, cause you're a full-growed white man. Maggie Green, you might a noticed, ain't that. She's only got two things she's good for. Housekeepin's one . . . " A lewd grin turned his lips. "An' if you don't know the second one . . . why, you ain't as full-growed as I thought you was."

Myron opened his eyes, folded his arms, grinned, arched an eyebrow. "You know," he said, "If I didn't know better, Mr. Treadwell, I'd suspect you done porked Maggie Green a time or two."

"More'n two, boy."

"Aw now, Mr. Treadwell . . . "

"I swear."

Myron pressed his lips together and cocked his head just a bit. "Well," he said, "if you don't mind me sayin so, sir—"

"What's your point, boy?"

"Well, it just don't seem—I mean it just sound like—"

"Sheeit. If you don't believe me, just ask Andy Fitts over to the post office. He'll set your dumb ass straight. Him and me and Orvy Still popped that bitch last . . . well I can't . . . must a been a couple of months back, anyway. Had her all night long, boy. Bitch couldn't walk right for a week, I reckon. Yeah, we got us some Wild Turkey and one a them—"

"Mr. Treadwell."

"What!"

"Mr. Fitts been dead four, five years now."

"You callin me a liar?"

"No sir, I ain't. It's just—"

"Well shut the fuck up then." Treadwell felt his lip trembling, fought against it. He stared hard at Myron, but the young man had apparently lost interest in their conversation. Myron stared at the countertop, dozy-eyed. He then looked under the counter, sat up, leaned forward, and began rooting through its shelves. He grabbed an old copy of *Sports Illustrated* and idly thumbed through it.

Threadwell felt his mouth move, felt words grumbling at the base of his throat. He really had no idea what he was going to say. He just felt the words boil up from his throat. His jaws felt stiff, as if he hadn't spoken for a decade, and then very slowly his words began to tumble from his mouth. "There's too goddamn many of em," he heard himself say. "There's too many niggers in this world, Myron. Them people breed faster'n jackrabbits. Ever damn place where you go there's niggers. In the front of buses. In restaurants. The goddamn federal gover'ments lettin em run all over the damn place. Hell, you can't even sit in a goddamn theater without thinkin that—that you could be sittin in a chair some coon warmed up for you durin the matinee. And what about them water fountains? Where's a body supposed to wet his whistle since they took down them signs downtown? . . . Well, I'm talkin to you, boy. Where the hell you supposed to go?"

He stood with his eyes bugging, his hand thrust forward. Myron sat and fanned himself with the magazine, a wing of red hair on top of his head, flapping up and down. Myron shifted in his chair and cleared his throat. "Don't nobody like none a this, but I, for one, ain't gonna thirst to death—"

"Well I sure would. I surely—"

"I mean, just so long as they don't try to mess with our women."

Treadwell threw his arms in the air as if signaling a touchdown, and then waved them. "There's the ticket, boy. Now you're sayin somethin. That's the next step, Myron. There it is. I'm telling you right now, that if you give a shit about your unborn daughter growin up in a world full a integratey, evil thinkin, black bucks . . . "

"Mr. Treadwell—"

" . . . help me string up Tossie Green an cut off his balls."

Treadwell dropped his arms. He leered at Myron, his tobacco-stained teeth glistening. Myron's eyes were big. "Help you?" said the young man.

"Tonight, boy. We can do it tonight, before his bitch gets home from my house."

"Lynch Tossie Green?"

"I didn't stutter, boy. Will you or won't you?"

"Tonight?"

"Yes. Tonight! Tonight! You a practicin retard, boy?"

At that moment the two men were startled by the growl of

an old truck. The sound shook the windows of the store. LouEllen sped into the store, red-faced and winded. "Treadwell. Theodore. You've got to come home."

No one would help him. No one understood.

Today, Myron had treated him as one would treat a madman. The way the boy cringed when he had spoken made him feel wild and helpless. "Where," he asked himself, "have all the men gone? What in God's name happened to all them fellers like Luke Parris and Erwin Cross. Now there was two white men could scare the black off tires just by clearin their throat." He sifted his mind again and again to conjure up the name of just one man who could help him turn the world right side up. He sifted and sifted till his head tightened, throbbed, burned. Just one. But none came. Only sepia images of the past tumbled through his mind. Images of black eyes that turned away from the sight of LouEllen's slender ankles, and the black lips shaping the word "sir," the day Uncle Pres pounded eight knuckles into the black face that would not yield enough sidewalk, the sable flesh he thrust himself into like day piercing night, the coiling, bouncing flames. . . . Just one word, just one name, please, just one sign. *Goddamit, Andy Fitts ain't dead. How could he be dead? Why, it was just a couple a months ago him and me and . . . who else was it was with us that night? All that Wild Turkey. Now who was it that night? Seems it was that redhead boy—*

Then his reverie was broken by the mewing of an infant. The two men leaped from their chairs and clambered into the living room. Tossie danced around the room in jubilation. "I'm a daddy!" he shouted. "Lord hell mercy, a daddy!" Treadwell slapped him on the shoulder and guffawed, "Let's go take a look at your youngun, Toss." He was relieved the child had not been stillborn, but was anxious to know of Maggie's condition. His legs felt like water. His head pounded. He thought he would vomit.

The men stumbled into the bedroom to find Maggie asleep, LouEllen sponging the newborn, and Clara tending to the afterbirth. Tossie stood frozen, staring at the baby. "It's a boy, Mr. Green." said Clara. "Ain't he just precious?" said LouEllen, as she swaddled the baby. "Well, don't be afraid of the child, Tossie, he doesn't even have teeth yet. Go on, son, hold your baby boy."

Tossie reached down, lifted the baby up into his great hands. He could have held him in the middle of his palm. "He sho is a pretty thing, Maggie. God Lord what a pretty child."

"Pretty's for girls, Tossie," said LouEllen. "That boy is handsome."

"I swear," said Treadwell. "Uh, looky here, Tossie, can I . . . why don't you let me hold him for a sec."

Tossie looked at LouEllen. She glanced at her husband, smiled at Tossie, and nodded. "You just see you careful wid im," said Tossie.

"I will, Toss. I'll be easy." Treadwell received the child into his arms, and Tossie knelt next to Maggie and stroked her brow. "Just what the world needs," thought Treadwell, "another goddamn pickaninny." He held the baby close to his chest and made cooing noises at him. He tried to smile, but this only made his head hurt more. He couldn't keep himself from trembling. A hot pressure surged through his chest, and his thoughts hissed at him, in a whirl of static, that if he were a man, he would dash the infant to the floor and kick it across the room. But almost as if Tossie sensed his thought, he rose, huge and heavy like a gathering storm, and stood close to Treadwell. "Howdy doo, youngun," said Treadwell, a little too loudly. The infant started and opened his eyes for an instant. The eyes seemed to shine a soft steel gray. "I'll be goddamned," Treadwell said. He hadn't intended to say it out loud. "What is it, Teddy?" demanded LouEllen, moving to her husband's side. Tossie stepped forward, making to seize the child. "What's wrong?" he said.

Treadwell stepped back from him. "Nothing's wrong, Toss. Just gimme a minute to hold him. I mean a ol . . . ol coot like me, well, it ain't ever day he gits to hold a darlin little boy like this here. Toss, you got the rest of your life with him. I just . . . I just want . . . " His voice dimmed to a whisper. "To look him over."

The room vibrated with a strange silence as Treadwell rocked the infant in his arms. "Howdy doo," he said. "Howdy doo," hoping the child would again open its eyes. Tossie, Clara, and LouEllen stood astonished as Treadwell rocked, cooed, smiled. He held the baby close to his chest, rocked him and rocked him. "Howdy doo, boy." He looked up from the baby into the unbelieving eyes of Tossie, moved toward him, placed the baby in Tossie's big arms and left the room.

As he lay in bed, this night, Theodore Treadwell felt reborn. He was happier than he had been in years. He was sure, sure as there would be a tomorrow, that there were other men in the world who saw things as he did. He wished for all his brothers, this night, just two things. First that they would rekindle the fires of the white race and rise up to tear the black world apart—cause black men were good for nothin. And black women were good for only two—no three, three things. Second. He wished that his brothers should someday know the sweet and unforgettable joy of holding their first born sons gently in their arms.

He hugged his pillow close to him, drifted into sleep, and dreamed of the fiery death of Tossie Green.

Previous Winners of the
Drue Heinz Literature Prize

The Death of Descartes, by David Bosworth, 1981
Dancing for Men, by Robley Wilson, Jr., 1982
Private Parties, by Jonathan Penner, 1983
The Luckiest Man in the World, by Randall Silvis, 1984
The Man Who Loved Levittown, by W. D. Wetherell, 1985
Under the Wheat, by Rick DeMarinis, 1986
In the Music Library, by Ellen Hunnicutt, 1987